THE BRE.
BEAUTY FOR ASHES

A Triumph of My Soul Anthology

COMPILED BY
AWARD-WINNING PUBLISHER ELISSA GABRIELLE

Peace in the Storm Publishing
Giving Your Soul a Rise...One Page at a Time

ISBN: 9798864875292

Peace in the Storm Publishing, LLC.
PO box 1152, Pocono Summit, PA 18346
Visit our Web site at **www.PeaceInTheStormPublishing.com**

Table of Contents

PUBLISHER'S NOTE

In the tapestry of human existence, adversity weaves its threads into the very fabric of our lives. It is a force that knows no boundaries, respects no privilege, and, at times, seems relentless in its pursuit. Yet, it is also within the heart of adversity that the indomitable spirit of resilience, courage, and strength emerges, like a phoenix rising from the ashes.

The pages you are about to turn hold stories of remarkable women who have faced adversity head-on, unflinchingly, and with an unwavering determination to triumph against all odds. Their narratives are a testament to the extraordinary power of the human spirit, but more specifically, the power of women to persevere and flourish even in the face of the most daunting challenges.

As we delve into the lives of these incredible women, we will discover that adversity is a universal experience, transcending geographic, cultural, and socio-economic boundaries. It is the great equalizer, proving that none of us are immune to its touch. But within these shared moments of adversity lies a profound truth – the potential for transformation, growth, and, ultimately, triumph.

Each of the women featured in this collection has forged her own path through the crucible of adversity. Their journeys are as diverse as the colors of the rainbow, yet the common thread that binds them together is their unwavering determination to rise above their circumstances, to redefine their destinies, and to inspire others with their tales of survival and success.

From the battered but unbroken spirit of the survivor to the visionary who shattered glass ceilings, from the single mother who defied society's expectations to the warrior who reclaimed her inner strength, these stories are a powerful testament to the resilience of the human soul and the remarkable capacity of women to overcome, adapt, and thrive.

In these pages, you will encounter stories of courage that will take your breath away, stories of perseverance that will move you to tears, and stories of hope that will rekindle the flame of possibility within your heart. These are stories that resonate with the struggles and aspirations of women everywhere, offering a beacon of hope in the darkest of hours.

In sharing their stories, these women not only celebrate their personal victories but extend a hand to every reader, inviting them to discover the strength within themselves to overcome their own adversities, big or small. They remind us that we are not defined by the challenges we face but by the way we rise above them.

As you embark on this journey through the pages of this book, may you be inspired, uplifted, and fortified by the indomitable spirit of these remarkable women. May their stories serve as a source of strength, guidance, and empowerment for all, regardless of gender, age, or circumstance. And may you, too, find the courage to turn adversity into your greatest ally, for within your own story, the seeds of triumph await.

With utmost admiration for these women of unwavering courage,

Elissa Gabrielle
Publisher

The Miseducation of a Black Girl
Armani Peterson

I felt an immense fear for what I was becoming... helpless, conformed, abused, and most importantly lost. I know what it is to be free. For the entirety of my life, I never allowed myself to be caged. But at this trajectory, I wasn't just caged, I was shackled to dance to the beat of Corporate America.

Underpaid, micro-aggression-filled, boundary obliterating Corporate America. Where my passion was depicted as aggression, my success and leading streak was a threat to the fragility that easily bonused on the back that broke to the conformity of their anger.

I was used and misused some would say. The better question is, had my eyes been the color of the ocean, hair easily danced in the breeze, and skin as light as the snowfall, would oppression have sought its way to me? Perhaps for me, I could've been in Corporate America, too. Where I would have led and those whose ancestors suffered to exist would lose. No need for violence, white women in this field are the new nice.

Anxiety, you have no place here, go to the bathroom and cry your mascara clear, pull yourself together, and don't let the inflection in your voice sell us the tone police who can't decipher rage over fear. They don't know what it is to feel lost, scared you won't be able to afford a car, your crib, or your dog, which is the only thing getting you through.

Not to mention the stress that made you lose 30 pounds in 10 days. You lost more than the weight of a man you thought was fate. But he can't see you for you now, he only sees what they have pushed out. A fear-bound, someone who is scared to leave the bed and cries when she leaves the house. A person whose smile would light up a room, but you've only seen tears for days.

Suddenly the days turned into months and all the lights stayed off. She puts on a mask for work; as soon as she returns, you see the hurt. They cut her pay and failed to mention they forgot to dock it. She has not seen a check in weeks searching through cabinets for something to eat. Having to decide if the dog gets to eat or me. I wasn't really hungry anyway. I don't want to call my parents though I know they'll pay. I just don't want to feel weaker than what I am. I put myself in this situation, how will I get out?

Depression are you winning? I don't want to feel something I can't name, this feeling here is something I can't explain. I cry when it's sunny, I cry when it rains. Anxiety has a hold of me, so I throw up night and day. I don't look in the mirror anymore because nothing fits my frame. I look so sick and why do I feel I'm the only person to blame? A slave mentally, I should've been madder at those who had betrayed me. All that time I spent mad at me.

See, but this little black girl was smart. She finally figured out how to play her cards. Because her mother warned her of her battle and the mother before her and she didn't want to continue their scars. In order for them all to heal. She would have to push and feel the sense of fighting back. Corporate America could lose to a lawyer fighting back. She had to possess all the facts. If the mistreatment, like being singled out because she was black. Being told she lacked emotional intelligence because what Corporate America defined as intelligence does fit the description of the skin I inherited, but oh boy how that fired back. This black girl brought chess to a checkers match.

Meet Armani Peterson

Hailing from Newark, New Jersey, Armani Peterson is an author, poet and spoken word artist. She has a love for the written word and artistic expressions.

Profoundly penning her first thoughts at the age of eight, Armani knows the power of words. A true humanitarian at heart, Armani's love for all things literary matches her love for people. Armani is a volunteer who works with those who are less fortunate. She also dedicates her time and efforts to support women who have been victims of domestic violence.

When Armani isn't volunteering to help those in need or performing spoken word, she is working on her first published full-length book of poetry and prose due to be released soon.

Roishina's Beauty for Ashes
Roishina Henderson

Stress Can Make You Sick

I had a blue-hour experience that lasted for several years. The blue hour is the darkest time just before sunrise, when the sky takes on an intense hue of blue. I was engulfed in the richest of that blue hour when my pockets were the poorest.
Let me tell you. Never be ashamed of the dark side of your life journey. You'll find beauty and strength like a rose rising through the cracks of concrete.

It's ideal and hopeful to have things figured out when we reach our upper thirties and especially into our forties. But sometimes, that's just when things can fall apart. But give yourself grace because it will all come back together.

I remember 2016 like it was yesterday. I had a mini mental breakdown. I cracked. Mentally. It was an overwhelming feeling I hadn't ever felt. I was stressed to the max after not finding work in my field, and my savings account had started to dwindle in big numbers. I'd had shouting matches of anger with God a few times. I was just at my wit's end, and then July 25 happened.

I felt tired. Mentally and physically. But more so physically, as I'd never experienced that level of fatigue before. I had a doctor's appointment later in the day. I was home taking a nap. When I woke up, it was like I still hadn't rested. I'd thought about canceling my appointment. But I forced myself to get up.

It was a summer day in Atlanta. I got into my Jeep and had the music and air conditioning blasting. I could only hear my music as I backed out of my driveway. But then I felt the crash and jumped out of the Jeep to investigate. "I was blowing my horn. You didn't hear me?" asked the guy I'd just collided with on my street.

I didn't. I observed the damage, and it was visible that there was a hit, but it was minor.

I waved my hands in the air and said, "It's whatever." He went on his way, and I didn't care. I got back into my Jeep and drove those three miles to the doctor's office.

When I got in the parking lot and got out of my Jeep, I kind of froze for a minute. A wave of deliriousness flooded me. It was at that moment, it felt like I had just lost my mind. I was overwhelmed with confusion, sadness, and worthlessness. I'd been sad before. Even some minor depression, but that wasn't depression— I didn't think. It wasn't sadness, it felt more like grief, except no one had died. Or maybe someone did at that moment: Me.

I managed to walk inside the doctor's office like a zombie. There were a couple of women in the office, but it felt like it was just me. I was checked in, took the clipboard of paperwork I had to fill out, and sat down with my head hung low. And that wave of deliriousness hit me again. And this time, I couldn't contain it. I cried in that chair. Hard. A part of me was so embarrassed, but I couldn't stop that wave of overwhelmingly sad feelings. I was then shaking, crying uncontrollably.

I can only imagine if I were watching someone else going through what I was, I'd think that person was having a mental meltdown, And I believe I was. I managed to get a handle on myself a few minutes later and filled out the paperwork. I'd found out I'd lost about twenty pounds, and I told the doctor about my fatigue feelings. She took some blood work and called me the next day. "Where are you?" the doctor asked.

"Home," I said.

"I need you to drop what you're doing and get to the hospital. Go to ER."

My glucose levels were reaching close to a thousand, according to her. I was diagnosed with Diabetic Ketoacidosis. I was clueless, but I was about to learn to deal with it, in the midst of a storm that had already been brewing.

That Call Center Life Teaches You

For the life of me, I couldn't understand why I was having the hardest time finding solid work. I had moderate success in my career field, but everything was a no, and I had applied for hundreds of jobs online.

I had a mortgage and a child. I didn't want to lose my house, so I had to do what was needed to stay afloat – even though I'd felt I drowned so many times.

"Are ya'll still hiring?" I remember asking as I went to a local call center. I got tired of being rejected for jobs via email. I'd decided it was time for me to go see some employers face-to-face. If I were to be told no, they would have to tell it to my face.

"We are. We're actually conducting interviews right now. Can you stick around?" A recruiter asked me.

I knew it was a low-wage job, but I'd never felt so good at that very moment. It was a feeling of finally having a full-time job again. The job paid nine dollars per hour, and training started at 6 a.m. I didn't care, I wanted to feel wanted. For a job! And though I did the math on bills versus pay, I knew I was still going to come up short. But I knew it's always easier to GET a job when you already HAVE one!

I think I lasted about a year on that job, only to go to another call center job for a couple more dollars an hour. Those call center jobs taught me about humility, having compassion for those who make little, and then taking that little and making much however they can.

Fast Cash

I had a Jeep Cherokee that got totaled some years back. A young girl jumped a lane trying to get to the gas station on Northside Drive in Atlanta when she crashed into me.

I got another Jeep, and that newer Jeep led me to make extra income since the call center job still wasn't making ends meet. I got curious about driving for Uber. Part of me was nervous about the thoughts of strangers being in my car, but the need for money mattered a tad more.

One Thursday night, I turned on the rideshare app. My mind was made up that I was going to devote Saturday to driving. But I wanted to do a test run to kinda shake the jitters off. Within a minute or two, I got a ping – a notification that someone needed a pickup. Without thinking too hard, I accepted the ride. The app was user-friendly, as I could see the pickup spot, and GPS guided me to the location.

I picked up two young ladies. That gave me some ease and it felt less intimidating. And it was even better that the drop-off was only about three miles away. When I confirmed drop off and saw my first pay, I was hooked. I took one more ride that night and made it home. I knew then I could do that job to help ends meet or to make some fast money.

On a Hamster's Wheel

My brother Rai has played a significant role in keeping me encouraged during my dark hours – stressing the importance of listening to God's voice and obedience. Otherwise, as he had put it I'd continuously "be on a hamster's wheel of running and going nowhere."

And boy, was I ever! But you know what? I eventually got off that wheel. Thank God!

Don't Auction My House or Repossess My Jeep

I was about in my fourth time going into home foreclosure. But this last go around on the foreclosure, things went a little differently. I fought to stay in my house. I loved that house. It was the perfect, two thousand square feet ranch house with three bedrooms and two bathrooms. It was low maintenance. I didn't bother my neighbors, and they didn't bother me.

I couldn't see myself living anywhere else, but I was in a season where I stayed strapped for cash. And though my mortgage payment was affordable to most, I struggled to stay afloat. I just wasn't making enough money with my part-time insurance job and rideshare driving. Crazy, right?

Nonetheless, I battled for that property by refinancing, writing letters, and always making payment arrangements. But as my brother reminded me, I was still a hamster on a wheel. But this last time, and although it appeared I was losing the battle, the war victory was mine.

The house was scheduled for an auction on December 5, 2017, on the steps of Fulton County courthouse. The day before the auction, I received a call about fifteen minutes before 5 p.m. when I received a call. I was driving in College Park, Georgia, and pulled into a church parking lot. The person informed me that the auction was being removed and other arrangements were going to be made for me to retain possession of the house. I knew it was nobody but God who worked that out. And thankfully, I hadn't dealt with another foreclosure since that time. As they say, "God may not come when you want him. But

He's always right on time."

Time with My Son Makes the Light Bulb Turn On
–The Shift–

For ten years, Wednesdays were my date nights with my son, Seth. In Spring 2022, I went to the Taco Mac restaurant in Stockbridge, Georgia. Seth would be heading into his senior year of high school that fall, and I wanted to talk about his plans for the future.

"Have you started thinking about college?" I asked.

"Yes," he said dryly, with zero interest in continuing the conversation topic.

"Well, now is the time to start thinking about your next move," I reminded him.

But this time, a light bulb went off in my head. What was going to be *my* next move? I was *still* in my blue hour of life, but I felt it was truly on me to begin to see a sunrise. I guess I'd known it was always on me, free will. But when you get fed up enough, you'll finally do what's beneficial for your life. At least, I'd hope for anyone. I knew then it was time I knew then it was time to talk with God about my placement in the future and where He sees me.

I'd always known my purpose. But somehow, I just couldn't make things happen in Atlanta, and I wanted it to. Why wouldn't I? My son was there, and I had roots in a house I loved, but something was tugging me again to move. Yeah, I'd had that feeling years prior, but I didn't consult God. I just did what I wanted to do. And that had proven to be fruitless.

However, that one dinner with my son lit a new fire—one I couldn't ignore and finally felt wise to explore. I did. And today,

I'm so glad I did.

I Had a Dream and a Conversation with God

I'm a dreamer. God deals with me through dreams. I could take a fifteen-minute nap, and I would have a dream about something. But the ones I feel where God is speaking stick out like a sore thumb.

So, one night, I had a dream. It was a dream where I was home in Mississippi. I was with a college friend, and we were walking in a backyard and came across two big dogs. I'm not typically afraid of dogs, but I was scared of these dogs. I tried to conceal my fear but ran a short distance and stopped. The dog wasn't trying to harm me; he wanted to love on me. The dream reminded me so much of familiar territory and that I needed to stop running. The dog felt like *home*, and home was where I was going to find my purpose. It was where I was to flourish and be on fertile grounds.

After that dream, I told God, "Yes to His will and way for my future." I asked Him for directions on how I needed to move forward on going back to my home state. A simple, *sincere* 'yes' makes a world of difference.

The Turnaround before the Turnaround

The morning after making up my mind about moving back home to Mississippi felt different. You know how, for some brides, the first dress they try on is *the* dress? That's how it was with this investor I was getting ready to sell my house to. He was my first contact to inquire about it. I entertained a few other investors, but I worked with the first guy.

At the time, the real estate market was in favor of the sellers, so I was able to get a generous offer. The arrangement allowed me to stay in the house for an extra month to pack up. I still had some reservations, though. I was leaving about seven months sooner than I really wanted to, but I wanted to capitalize on the market by selling the property.

I attempted to find an apartment until the following spring. Don't you know I had the hardest time trying to find an apartment in Atlanta? Though I had the proceeds from the house sale, property management companies still only used my income at the time to determine if I could get an apartment. And sadly, I didn't make the minimum of forty thousand annually. I just barely made half of that. I was met with closed door after closed door of securing a place, and I had to be out of the house by the end of August.

On the day of my birthday in mid-August, I treated myself to my favorite entertainer, Michael Bublé, in Tampa, Florida. I stayed in a nice river-view-facing hotel at The Embassy.

While there, I spoke to my brother about the challenges I faced while trying to stay in Atlanta for another few months.

"Go home," he demanded. He'd had a few other firm but loving choice words, too. We laughed, but he was absolutely right about not waiting to go home. His words were what I needed to hear, so I'd chosen to go back home and go back sooner than planned.

That one roadblock that summer of not finding an apartment didn't make sense until months later.

I Got So Much Beauty Now

I was born and raised in Greenwood, Mississippi. So, I returned home to focus on writing full-time – my God-given purpose – the thing God had been trying to redirect. the thing God had been trying to redirect--. The cause of my blue hour, which lasted several years, was that I stayed stuck in disobedience to God.

Amazingly, a change of location can set your new path on fire, and that's exactly what happened. While in Atlanta, I started writing a few things but could never finalize those writing projects, and I had three books I wanted to complete.

It felt amazing to be home again from day one. It was a natural fit, one I wasn't so sure about. On that warm September day in 2022 when I pulled up to the house – the house I grew up in – I got out of my car and soaked it all in. The first thing I heard was blues music blasting about a block away.

"I'm home," I said.

Your Blessings Will Find You

I've always been a God believer, but within a year, God had truly shown Himself to me. I had a plan to maximize the time spent at my parents' home to finish writing my books, but God created an opportunity for me.

One day, I went to my social media business page to update that I'd had a new writing business. A former colleague reached out to me when she saw I was online.

I called her, and she mentioned that she needed a new editor on her team. I couldn't believe what I was hearing. My mind immediately went to God, asking "What are you doing here?" The position was contract-based and remote, with a lucrative compensation package. My mind was blown.

"Ask for what you want," she advised me on the salary. I could've fallen off the bed. And so, I did. Things moved so quickly. I was offered the job, and I indeed asked for what I wanted. Six figures.

Wait a minute, God? For more than five years, I desperately looked for work in my field, and I always came up empty. Here it was, I was back in my hometown in less than three months and found career work to be an editor for a major corporation.

That roadblock on not finding an Atlanta apartment? It then made sense why I couldn't find a place to stay in Atlanta just a few months prior. I would've missed out on that career opportunity to be an editor. I know I would've never gone to my business social media page to update it had I still been in Atlanta because there wouldn't have been a new business at *that time* to share. My former colleague would've never found me, and I would've missed that career train.

One would think that the plan to finish my books would've slowed me down by taking on a new full-time job. No, it really just fueled my fire to complete my books. And not just one book at a time; I was determined to finish all three books together. Why? I wanted to honor God.

I knew it was nobody but God who'd opened those opportunities to be able to successfully sell my Atlanta property and position me to fulfill my purpose in writing.

God gave me such beauty for the ashes of everything that I'd ever suffered and sacrificed. And honestly, the grace for my disobedience.

The Lesson I Learned

When you know and understand the purpose of your life, the way is already made for you to succeed. Will there be challenges? Possible. It's life. None of us are exempt from life's struggles. But I have learned that life can be smoother when you yield to God's purpose for your life.

Ever since the day I told God 'Yes to His will, there has been open door after open door and a resounding 'yes' from Him. Your blessings – expected and the unexpected – will chase you. The blessings will find you! God does restore and will give more than double for the troubles you may experience.

Those years of being in the valley – that blue hour – I wouldn't trade it for anything. I walked away with natural blessings. But more importantly, it built my character, compassion for people, and trust in God.

Don't wait years to get your life on track for your life's calling. I believe the Bible when it says, "Your gifts will make room for you." I'm a living testimony of that right now.

I know now that I don't have to skip chapters of my life to know what's up ahead. I trust God.

I already know the end is victorious. The blue hour has passed. I'm basking in the sunshine of my life's purpose.

Meet Roishina Henderson

She has written over 500 published news articles and has authored four books. She also has more than ten years of experience in professional communications with major city governments and corporations.

Roishina is currently an editor for a major wireless network company.

The Mississippi native is involved with community theater in her hometown, where she's looking forward to making her directorial debut for a stage play in early 2024. She's also working on her 5th novel, a gripping tale of her family's story, while helping others publish their books.

Roishina continues to do inspirational blogging on her website at **roishina.com**.

Unbreakable Love: A Mother's Journey Through Heartbreak and Healing
Cheryl Lacey Donovan

I struggled to put pen to paper for this one. As a minister, I found solace in guiding others toward spiritual enlightenment. However, my greatest challenge lay within my own home, where my adult son battled the relentless storms of bipolar disorder and addiction. The first time I wrote about my journey as a mother, I had yet to experience the devastation that can take place when one of your children travels to the brink of extinction. I remember clearly saying on more than one occasion that I had no idea what I would do if God asked me to sacrifice one of my sons the way He asked Abraham to do in Genesis 22. Well, suffice it to say that I know exactly what I would do now.

It all began ten or twelve years ago. Time escapes me now because so much has happened. It feels like a lifetime ago. I was that Mama who took pride in involving herself in every aspect of her children's lives. "Pride," now that's an interesting word. Scripture says, "It goes before a fall." But I digress. I am and always was a good parent, even without a handbook. I prayed and did all the "so-called" right things. I was guided by specialists and believed in them. I made sure I knew about all the childhood diseases, but no one ever told me about the one that was more silent than others. The one that can take a child's life from you without you even knowing it — the disease of addiction. It creeps into your life, affects your entire family, and leaves you with pain and loss. My son, in his late 20s, was a wonderful young man. He was the kind of son every mother dreams of — caring and loving; he would do everything and anything to help you. He would always go that extra mile. He can make you laugh when you're down or sit and hold your hand when things get rough.

Then, he began to use drugs and alcohol. I am ashamed to admit that there may have been signs in his early college years, but I never expected his issues to be as severe as they turned out to be years later. I chalked his behavior up to college antics. After all, several young adults go over the proverbial "fools hill," right? Therefore, I justified it in my mind that there was no harm in it. By the time my youngest turned 25, he was back home and had a year or so to complete his bachelor's degree. His reason for coming home, or so he told me, his brother had graduated, and he would now be by himself at the University. They had gone there a year apart to some local fanfare because one was a basketball player and one a football player attending the same college campus. Now, his brother was done, and he was there alone. I was in a conundrum; on the one hand, I wanted him to stay so he could finish. Yet, on the other hand, I wasn't sure how he would navigate by himself with no family there. After all, even with his brother there, he indulged in questionable activity. He tried to continue classes to no avail. He even got a job, but none of It lasted very long. There were new people I had never heard of before or ever seen. My son no longer had any of his childhood friends around, nor did he keep in touch with them. He was irritable, moody, and melancholy. He would rarely eat, and when he did, he would binge eat everything in sight until he was sick to his stomach. He would sleep all day and be up all night. Of course, I justified him being up all night as a night owl. He fancied himself a rapper, which was not bad, in and of itself, but looking back, it may have been part of his delusions of grandeur.

The rubber met the road one day when my son was outside talking with my husband's cousin. My husband's cousin smashed a can on the street in front of our house and for whatever reason that act attracted the police who were already in our neighborhood (A whole 'nother story). That one event kicked off a train wreck that caused us to be derailed for over ten years. My son had a small amount of marijuana on him, so the police took him in. He also had a warrant for a traffic violation. Several days later, he was released and was in a state I had never seen before. When I first saw him, my legs became weak, and I thought I would pass out right there, but I knew I needed to maintain my composure as much as I could to assist him. On the surface, I thought the police had done something to him. I would soon learn he was experiencing withdrawal from prescription medication that was not his to take.

To circumvent the rules, he began using this synthetic stuff that took him in an unexpected direction that we're still trying to figure out. When my son is under the influence, there are no boundaries. He becomes a person I don't even know. Sometimes, even his facial expression changes, and I barely recognize who he is at that moment. I watched a beautiful child grow from a sweet, innocent bundle of joy to a mischievous little boy doing all the things little boys do. Never in my wildest dreams did I ever think that one day, a horrible disease would strike this child and turn him into someone completely different. We took him home and thought the worst was over. In our minds, we would move on from this setback and get on with our lives. NOT! I found myself plummeting into a foray of scenarios I thought I never would encounter, but, if I'm honest, I had seen them before in his father. However, back then, no one spoke of mental illness, self-medicating, or anything remotely related to that, especially in the African-American community. It was a new road, one plagued with excuses, misunderstandings, and sheer fear for my child's life. I was trying to manage my son's mental illness and drug use. Of course, I would ask him "ARE YOU USING DRUGS?" And, of course, he would reply, "NO!" He would have a multitude of excuses. Pathetically, I would buy into the BS he was selling and once again believe what he was saying, and once again, I would TURN A BLIND EYE.

It became a vicious cycle. My heart ached each time he slipped into the abyss of his mental episodes. The raw emotions I felt were a whirlwind of fear, helplessness, and profound sadness. My tears often flowed as I watched him grapple with his inner demons, wishing I could shield him from the torment that consumed his mind.

I can recall him being the focus of my attention and energy since he was in a bad way, spiraling out of control and plummeting to the ground. He was well on his way to a deep, dark black hole filled with drug addiction and total despair. There were so many signs that I should have paid attention to, But I WAS IN TOTAL DENIAL. I made a plethora of excuses for him and found myself defending him relentlessly. Balancing my role as a minister with my son's struggles was an excruciating task. I worried about the judgment of others, fearing that their perceptions of my perfect ministerial image would be tarnished by my son's battles. I questioned whether I had failed as a mother, doubting my ability to provide the love and support he needed.

This whole dilemma would create total chaos and tension within our home as we faced an unrelenting storm caused by our youngest son's mental illness and addiction. My oldest watched as his once vibrant brother spiraled out of control. He struggled with mixed feelings of concern, frustration, and helplessness as he saw his little brother's destructive choices.

My oldest son also recognized that his brother made conscious decisions that exacerbated his problems. He believed he needed to take responsibility for his actions and face the consequences rather than relying on me to rescue him every time. Despite his worry, my eldest couldn't deny the reality that the lifestyle choices his brother was making were wreaking havoc for everyone involved.

I struggled to balance my love for my baby with the need to let him face the repercussions of his actions. My older son often found himself in disagreements with me because he urged me not to enable his addictive behavior any longer. He believed that my youngest needed to confront the consequences of his actions to truly understand the gravity of his situation.

Meanwhile, my husband felt caught in the crossfire. He loved our son as if he were his own, but the constant unpredictability of his mental episodes made him uneasy and fearful. My husband grappled with a difficult dilemma: to express his concerns and risk driving a wedge between him, myself, and our youngest, or to keep quiet and watch the turmoil unfold.

As the storm raged on, the family's dynamics grew strained. The baby boy's outbursts, often directed at my husband, created an atmosphere of tension and anxiety within the household. His love for our youngest boy clashed with his frustration at his choices, leaving him emotionally torn.

I didn't make matters any better. I would make numerous idle threats, of course, but never enforce what I would demand. I would pay the court fines as opposed to him going to jail. I would even go as far as to secure an attorney, after all, he was in hot water. I would pay for tickets, and car accidents, and even obtain an apartment because I didn't want him to be homeless. He later walked away with no explanation. In short, I did whatever I could to make my son's life easier so he would not have to endure the hardships and consequences. I had become the ULTIMATE CODEPENDANT MOTHER. Truth be known, I was just as sick as my son. For years, I blamed myself, wondering if my actions or choices had somehow triggered my son's condition. The guilt weighed heavily on my heart, and I questioned my worthiness as both a mother and a spiritual guide. I often found myself praying for answers, seeking divine guidance to understand why my son had to endure such hardships.

It was several years before my medical instincts kicked in and I began to seek help from mental health professionals. My son was not just an addict, he suffered from mental health issues. I remember scoffing at the thought when the doctor mentioned it in his first encounter after the can-smashing incident. But it was now very apparent that all of this was his way of dealing with the confusion of what was in his mind.

Mental health is still very taboo. No one understood. Everyone believed that this was something he chose, therefore, he could control it. Parents: Believe me when I tell you that the roller coaster ride is unbelievable. The pain you endure is unimaginable, yet the world expects you to go on like nothing has happened. Families are hurt, and those who don't understand addiction are always quick to put you down or to place blame. I have learned that until you comprehend the truth, you cannot find peace within yourself, or be able to help your child who is struggling with addiction. Accepting the reality, and proceeding from there, allows you to help both yourself and your child. I do not hate my son for using substances and for putting all of us through this pain. I hate the disease of addiction and the things he does because of it. I hate lying and stealing. I love my son very much, but I hate his ways, and, it is perfectly okay, and necessary, to separate the two.

How does the mother of an addict cope? How does she juggle the incomprehensible challenge of supporting a loved one by not enabling their habit? And how does she deal with the stigma of having a child who is an addict? Well, let me make it clear. Being the mother of an addict is an incredibly lonely and isolating place, and often, the only people who understand what they're going through are other mothers who are going through it themselves. I feel deep empathy toward parents just beginning the terrible journey of their child's addiction — and those facing the turmoil of a potential next step: rehab, incarceration, or considering dislodging your child from the family home. Examples like these are still painful for me. We have learned and faced several difficult lessons throughout our journey, all of which we previously denied in the beginning. It didn't matter who was telling us the truth because we thought we knew better. After all, he is our son. We have come to accept these truths, and today it is much easier to deal with heartache. We have become more effective at helping our son through addiction, and much more effective at helping ourselves through the process.

It has been a long journey — a long, winding road on a path to the unknown. But one day, as I sat on the deck, listening to the water flowing from our backyard pond, a revelation struck me like a bolt of lightning. I realized that mental illness was not a result of my actions or shortcomings. It was a complex interplay of genetics, environment, and circumstances that I had no control over. With this newfound clarity, I began a journey of self-forgiveness and acceptance.

As a family, we now take it one day at a time. I can honestly say that I am much better at not organizing other people's lives, co-signing their chaos, cleaning up their messes, trying to control an outcome, or interfering with their journey. I am learning that I cannot control people, places, or things and I can only control my thoughts and actions. I joined support groups and connected with other parents who faced similar challenges. Through shared stories and empathetic conversations, I learned that I was not alone in my struggle. As I began speaking to friends and congregation members, I discovered a wellspring of compassion and understanding I never expected.

I am so grateful to be able to share my experience regarding my son's addiction. Writing it down on paper (which I have never done), became much more real to me and enabled me to see my part in my son's addiction as well as the complete insanity and dysfunction we have been living in. I had become so accustomed to this way of living that I was complacent and OKAY with the craziness and insanity.

Over time, my love for my son has transformed into an

unbreakable force, undeterred by the storms that rage within him. I have embraced my role as both a mother and a minister, using my experiences to offer guidance and support to others facing similar trials. Through my vulnerability, I have become a beacon of hope, proving that love can withstand even the darkest of times.

In the end, my painful journey has led her to a place of healing and empowerment. I have realized that my love for my son has not been defined by his illnesses, and my strength as a minister has not been diminished by the challenges my family faced. My story has become a testament to the resilience of the human spirit, a reminder that love and compassion can overcome even the most formidable obstacles.

And so, my story continues to inspire and uplift, a testament to the power of a mother's unwavering love and the transformative journey toward self-acceptance and healing.

Meet Cheryl Lacey Donovan

An award-winning bestselling author, speaker, mentor, and entrepreneur, Cheryl has influenced the lives of thousands in the U.S. and abroad through her powerful life-changing messages.

Cheryl is uniquely positioned to impact the lives of individuals she comes in contact with for long-term success with her message of faith and powerful vision of bringing purpose into the people equation to promote happier, healthier more meaningful life experiences.

Choose to Arise
Sherabim Joy

What do you do when the touch of your finger seems to yield waterfalls of grief and not rivers of greatness? How do you hold on to the positive affirmations that have been spoken into your spirit by those who see the magnitude of your future victories despite the present echo of defeat ricocheting throughout every aspect of your life? The answer is simple yet bathed in truth and wisdom. The answer is that you must make a choice. You must choose to either succumb to the deceptive lies whispering failure into your hearing or you must choose to have an honest conversation with yourself and with God regarding your situation. If you choose the latter, understand that your dialogue must include confession and acceptance of where you played a leading role in the drama and chaos of your life. Admitting your mistakes and acknowledging them will help you to readjust your mindset, giving you the courage to confidently try again.

I know this to be true, not because I'm a professional on the subject matter, but because I walked this exact path on my journey to recalibrating and resuscitating my vision, my passion, and my determination to become the woman of confidence and accomplishment that I was ordained to become. It was not an easy process. Truthfully, I am still traveling this road to inner healing, and it is still a challenging experience. I have shed many tears, and I expect many more to stream from my eyes in the coming days.

Sleepless nights, driven by worry, depression, and regret, are part of my story. However, I believe my story's conclusion will be marinated in triumph and victory. My struggles don't define me. My struggles have empowered me to pursue my purpose.

There was a period in my life when I went through a perpetual cyclone of disappointment, insurmountable stress, heartbreak, and humiliation. As a preacher of the Gospel of Jesus Christ, I could not understand why I seemed to be living the opposite of the joyous life in Christ that I regularly preached and taught about. I felt like a swimmer stranded in the middle of an ocean struggling helplessly to not be swept away by its salty torrent waves. Life was tough, and it was hard for me to keep my head held high. The fairytale life I had dreamed of from childhood was far from my reality.

The last decade of my life has been a whirlwind. It seemed like I could not do anything right. What I initially thought were blessings, in time, revealed to be nothing more than demons disguised as angels of light. The shame of the foreclosure on my first home loomed over my head as menacingly as starving ravens over a pile of carcasses. I refused to talk about it, and instead, I internalized my anger and disappointment at being the first in my immediate family to lose my home.

I tried to save my home, but it became impossible because, in 2008, I made the mistake of getting involved in predatory lending and ended up owing more on my property than it was worth. I attempted a mortgage modification and a short sale which was almost my saving grace, but at the last minute, the deal fell through. Finally, I succumbed to the struggle, accepting that the property wasn't worth saving. The foreclosure was a long and draining process that spanned several years and haunted me daily. At that time, I considered it the biggest failure of my life. I did not think I could be humiliated anymore. That is until I met the man that I chose to marry a few years later.

I was in my late 30's and desperately wanted a husband, children, and a home. I had been dating a man, on and off, for several years, and I always thought that I would eventually marry him. We would break up and then we would reconcile.

Truthfully, we had our issues, but I always assumed we would work them out and get married. Unfortunately, after our last breakup, in my heart, I knew that it wasn't going to happen. I cared very deeply for him, so I was devastated when it didn't work out. I was at a place of vulnerability. Two weeks after I broke up with him, I met the man I would later marry.

My pastor always says, "Never go grocery shopping when you're hungry." If you go grocery shopping when you're hungry, you will buy the first thing that you see to satisfy your ravenous appetite. Clearly, I was emotionally and socially starving when I settled into my next relationship which turned into marriage.

I always said that I would marry a man like my father. Robert Lee Allen is not only my father, but also my hero and one of my closest friends. To this day, my dad can do no wrong in my sight and I would fight to the death for him. I have always admired his strength, perseverance, love, and commitment to our family. I expected the same when I started my own family, but because I made the wrong choice, I experienced the exact opposite.

It was a beautiful day, September 8, 2012, when we exchanged vows, and we started our lives together. I had happily planned all the intricate details of our wedding ceremony and reception. Purple was my favorite color; it represented royalty and wealth, which I believed my marriage would yield. My wedding party was beautiful and traditional, with several bridesmaids, groomsmen, matron of honor, maid of honor, flower girl, and ring-bearer all dressed in our royal color scheme. The Salt Covenant, signifying our eternal unity and devotion to one another, was performed, and an anointed prayer of longevity and blessings prayed over us.

If only the joy, I experienced on September 8th was enough to carry us through the days following the ceremony. After spending $10,000 on our wedding, we had about six months of blissful happiness. Shortly afterward, the problems started and never stopped. Dreams of a happily ever after faded like a colorful cape drenched in bleach. Financial stress, infidelity, lies, deception, disrespect, emotional and mental abuse, and lack of support plagued our marriage. We separated three times in less than five years. I tried to make the marriage work. I suggested marital counseling, but my husband refused to go. I fasted, and I prayed. I prayed, and I fasted. However, the marriage continued to deteriorate as the rust of broken trust continued to eat away at its fiber. After months of struggling, I realized that I was the only one in the relationship committed to saving it. Emotional exhaustion does not adequality describe the strain and pain that I contended with daily. My weight dropped by 30 pounds one year and then several months later ballooned up to record pounds because of emotional eating.

Daily tasks became a chore because I was drenched by despair and debilitated by depression. I had reached a place where I lacked the energy to continue to fight for someone who refused to fight for me. So, when my husband asked me for a divorce, my response to him was, "I am going to give you what you've asked for."

If I continued to attempt to salvage the relationship, I probably would have experienced a nervous breakdown. I needed healing, but I would not be able to receive it while my soul was still intertwined with the source of its trauma, my husband. I never thought that I would end up becoming a divorcee. Once again, I found myself needing to make a tough choice. This time, I made a good one. I chose me and my son, so I took the lead, which was the norm in my marriage, and decided to end things with my husband. Dressed in disgrace, I filed for divorce. It felt like I was living in an alternate reality, and I found the entire experience numbing. My heart ached, but I knew with all my being that I was making the right decision for my sanity.

I was heartbroken and confused but I kept busy to

counteract the negative thoughts that I was tormented by. My mind frequently deceived me into believing that others were pointing their fingers at me and silently whispering *I told you so.* The reality was that I was surrounded by a supportive community that was praying and rooting for me. There were days that I could barely hold my head up because my spirit had become soaked with depression and my eyes were too weary from crying to see the beauty of freedom that the divorce had granted to me. I was devastated and it took me years to arise from the ashes, but I did finally arise.

Before I could fully cope with the divorce and being flung into single motherhood, I was stung with the arrow of back-to-back job lay-offs. In addition, I was forced to move from one home rental to another for several reasons. Some moments seemed to asphyxiate me. Bouts of anxiety had become normal, with my thoughts racing faster than a driver hitting the wall on a speedway and spinning out of control. Somehow, I managed to function during this journey of darkness, cleverly fooling my close friends and loved ones into believing that I was all right when, the truth was, I contended daily with frequent suicidal thoughts. I continued to preach. I continued to teach. I continued to write books, but I was drowning in sorrow. I thank God for my young son, Emmanuel. He was my inspiration. I had to live to make sure that he had a good life.

For quite a while, I foolishly chose to suffer in silence because I didn't want my image marred. In public arenas, I portrayed a woman of strength and confidence, but privately, I was an emotional disaster. I was not in a healthy state mentally, emotionally, or spiritually and I was keenly aware of it. I wasn't happy, but I wanted to be. I wasn't well, but I wanted to be whole. I reached a point where I had nothing left to give anyone other than myself. It was a place of selfishness, but it was a place of necessity. I had just enough strength remaining to start my journey to total health and well-being.

I've learned a lot on this journey. One of the most valuable lessons that I have learned is that true wellness does not occur independently or by chance. Wellness requires intentionality, participation, and assistance. I concluded that my wellness was my choice and that I needed to put in the work to become whole and healed.

The first thing I did was to have an honest conversation with myself and God regarding all the events that had transpired in my life. I prayed, and I did a deep dive into the core of my soul. I asked God to "show me...me". What I discovered was eye-opening and humbling. I was confronted with the truth. The truth was that a lot of my failures were due to my poor decisions. I realized that these poor decisions were rooted in the depth of my low self-esteem. Yes, I was a motivational speaker, and yes, I was an anointed, powerful, and effective preacher. Yes, I was a leader of youth and women in my local worship assembly, and yes, I was a mentor to many. Yes, I was a multi-time published author, and yes, my self-esteem was in the toilet. I did not believe in myself or understand my worth and value. Had I truly believed I deserved better, I would have certainly made different choices. I settled for less simply because I did not think that I was worthy to receive more.

Not only that, most of the decisions I made did not even line up with the scriptures that I preached from. I did not seek God before I made the decisions; I did what seemed logical and convenient at the time. Had I genuinely sought God, waited for Him to answer, and followed His instructions, I know I would have made different choices.

I've learned a lot on this journey. One of the most valuable lessons that I have learned is that true wellness does not occur independently or by chance. It requires intentionality, participation, and assistance. I concluded that my wellness was my choice and that I needed to do the work to become whole and healed. Many of my poor choices were a result of not doing proper research, asking the right questions, seeking wise counsel, and waiting for the right opportunities. I had established an unhealthy pattern of settling for the first thing that came my way and/or for what people said I was eligible to have. I realized that I did not understand my worth. Had I embraced my value, I would never have invested in my first property. In retrospect, that property did not even come close to the vision I had written out; but I settled for it. Shame on me, for settling for a dump. What is the point of writing a vision if you don't believe that faith and hard work will cause that vision to become a reality?

I started asking myself some tough questions. Why did I choose to settle for a property beneath my expectations? I settled for it because I did not believe that I deserved better. The bank dictated my eligibility, and I fell for their estimation of my worthiness. Had I truly believed in my future, I would have dismissed their offer, saved more money, improved my credit, and sought funding elsewhere instead of settling. In the end, settling will only lead to dissatisfaction and distress.

How many times in your life can you say that you are guilty of the same thing? Have you ever accepted people's estimation of your abilities instead of requiring yourself to dismiss their opinions and push yourself to your greatness? Have you ever settled in a relationship, career, home, or position because that was the best offer that came your way? Listen, and repeat after me," I am worth more." You do not need to settle. You must believe in yourself and wait for the best, knowing you deserve the best. I urge you to wait. Not until a *better* opportunity comes along, but until the *right* opportunity presents itself.

Now, let's discuss my marriage. Before I continue, I would like to share that I now have a cordial relationship with my ex-husband. We work together to raise our son, and I will always appreciate and commend him for it. I would never intentionally disrespect him or present him as a villain. We just did not work out together as husband and wife. There will always be a level of love in my heart for him because he is the father of my child and I wish him nothing less than the life of prosperity and success that God has for him.

As aforementioned, I always expected to marry a man like my handsome father. Had I truly believed I deserved a husband as amazing as him, I would have continued to wait despite the loud and obnoxious ticking of my biological clock. My father was raised in a broken home. For a short time, he lived with his father, who suffered from alcoholism, but ended up being raised by his grandmother. He did not meet his biological mother until he was 19 years old. My dad made a personal vow to himself that he would never allow his children to experience the harsh life that he did. He was determined to provide a home filled with stability and love for his three daughters and one son. My dad kept his promise to himself and to us and made sure we all stayed together. He worked two jobs to provide for us, not requiring my mom to work so she could stay home to raise us. He was always a source of reliability. Even in my adulthood, when life is tough just being in my father's presence and hearing his voice comforts me to know that everything will be alright.

Now, travel back in time with me to the beginning of my relationship with my husband. Was he tall, caramel complexion, and handsome? Yes, he was. Was he available? Yes, he was. Did he express a genuine interest in me and shower me with adoration and attention? Yes, he did. Did he say and do the right things to win my heart and loyalty? Absolutely. Was he nice and kind to me? Yes, he was, and honestly, he still is at times. Now for the harder questions. Was he my soul mate? No, he was not, and I knew it. Was he the diamond that I always dreamed of marrying? No, he was not. He sparkled during the courtship, but I quickly learned that his sparkle was not quite as brilliant as a genuine diamond. It was more like that of cubic zirconium. He shined in the light of the sun, and its rays perfectly kissed his countenance during happy times. However, during challenging times the brilliance dimmed. During the dating process, I became aware of his difficulty in handling adverse situations, yet I married him anyway.

When the marriage failed, I had to ask myself some pointed questions concerning how I truly saw myself. I realized that once again, I yielded to that seven-letter word that has now become "*taboo*" to me; I *settled*. I settled because, in the depth of my heart, I did not truly view myself as attractive or appealing enough to marry the type of man I was hoping to marry.

Growing up, I was never the girl that most boys wanted to date. I was the "friend," or the one boys saw as a nice girl but whom they had no romantic interest. My sisters, on the other hand, experienced the opposite. They frequently caught the eyes of eligible single young men. I developed a complex, convincing myself that something was wrong with me. I didn't speak about it often, but I buried my true opinion of myself deep within the reservoir of my soul. I stopped liking myself because I believed that I was unlikable.

For years I was imprisoned in the mental comparison trap. I viewed myself through the eyes of the success stories of my siblings as well as my contemporaries. I did not feel as if I measured up so I "married down." The result was me vowing my eternal love to a man who nonchalantly played with my heart as carelessly as a toddler would a toy he no longer valued. At the end of the day, I concluded that my husband did not desire me.

When you genuinely love someone, you handle them delicately with the utmost care and concern. You don't treat them as if their presence in your life doesn't matter, and that's how my husband treated me. I'll never forget that day when I came to that realization; to say that I was overcome by pain and shame is an understatement. I remember a cascade of tears that lasted for weeks. I would wake up crying. I would get up from my desk at work and would retreat into the ladies' room to prevent from breaking down in front of my coworkers. I would drive home from work crying. The more I cried, the more it hurt because I kept reliving this realization. Anxiety crushed my core, and I started taking homeopathic anti-anxiety remedies. I was close to requesting prescription medication, but thankfully I was able to come out of the darkness before it resorted to that.

I needed help because I could not move beyond the shame and self-loathing, I had for myself because of failing again. I lost my house, and now I was losing my marriage. Going to church was not working. My spirit was too broken to pray. I had no desire to preach or teach anyone anything. It was either get help or die. Dying was not an option. I had to live for Emmanuel. My baby boy needed me. I needed to push for his sake, so, what did I do? I did what most African American Christian women refuse to do; I sought professional counseling. Yes, this preacher paid a therapist to help her heal and travel the road of the overcomer. I can proudly say that I finally made a good decision.

Working with a therapist provided the avenue necessary to express my feelings in a safe environment without fear of judgment. I could cry and release my anger towards my husband and myself. I could sit and listen to the therapist say to me that "it wasn't my fault." I desperately needed to hear those words spoken aloud. I could sit and receive wise counsel from someone trained to understand the human psyche and emotions. Therapy helped me address how I ended up in the situation that I was in, and it helped me to heal and move forward, ensuring that I would never again revisit this place of bondage. It also allowed me to accept my humanness, my flaws, and successes, as well as my failures. Therapy reminded me that I was not the only one on the planet that had been stung by the "bee of life." Others have suffered the loss of homes and were able to recover. Others have suffered from the pain of divorce and are healed from it. Others survived and thrived, and I learned that I could, too.

Let me pause from my story for a moment and encourage you to take an introspective look at yourself. May I ask you, what challenges are you facing? Can you honestly say that you are navigating through life in a spirit of wholeness, or are you carrying a load of shame and hurt? Is depression taking over your life? If so, please do not suffer in silence when help is available. My philosophy is this; if the body can get sick…so can the mind. If we are unashamed to visit a primary care doctor for our physical ailments, why do we shy away from professionals trained to heal the mind when the pressures and stresses of life weigh on it? Don't allow pride to imprison you as I did for so many years. Make a choice. Seek help and start your journey to wellness. Remember what I said earlier, wellness does not occur independently or by chance. It requires intentionality, participation, and assistance. You are only alone if you choose to be. Make a good choice. Make the right choice and get help.

I have shared with you some of the biggest challenges that I have faced in my life because of poor choices. Now, let's fast-forward to the present and discuss some good ones that I have made that have allowed me to soar above my previous difficulties and land on the trail of triumph.

So, what is Triumph of My Soul? The triumph of my soul is that I have chosen to recover. I accepted responsibility; I was not dealt a bad hand…but rather I *chose* a bad hand. I took the lessons that I learned about myself during my season of trials, and I decided to reconstruct my view of myself. Having the right view empowered me to make better choices for myself, my son, and our future. There will always be challenges, but I know that I have the power to pivot, and so do you.

We've discussed my past, but now it's time to shift the dialogue and discuss my present and future. My story continues to unfold, and chapters of my life continue to be written one day at a time:

Chapter 1: Regaining My Vision

I regained my vision as a writer and released my first children's book, *"Manny and The Magic Keys,"* in 2020. I am so proud of the success of this book series. We developed a *"Gift A Book"* program. Over 300 books were sponsored by corporations and individuals and donated to schools and youth programs. Proceeds from the book sales were donated to my son's future college fund. Additionally, the book was read to over 300 children during the 2021 *"Read Across America"* national initiative. Lastly, In the Spring of 2023, season 1 of "Manny and The Magic Keys", animated series debuted on YouTube. The cartoon series has been well received and we look forward to continuing to develop new episodes.

Chapter 2: Resurrection of Ministry & Mentorship

I have rediscovered my love for ministry and mentorship, and I have been privileged to minister the Gospel of Jesus Christ at several locations virtually, in New Jersey and abroad. Over the past several months I have been told that I minister on a different level. I've been questioned about what has changed in my preaching. I simply smile, knowing that my pain has pushed me to a place of confidence about who I am in Jesus Christ, and people's opinions of me no longer imprison me. I preach authentically, passionately, and confidently.

Chapter 3: Corporate Career

In 2021, I was promoted to the position of Planning Manager. I had been struggling to advance in corporate retail for many years. Hard work, focus, favor, and prayer opened up the door to advancement.

Chapter 4: New Home Purchase

Recovery from foreclosure is possible! During the summer of 2021, I closed on a modest 3-bedroom one-family home for my son and me in the suburbs which boasts an A+ school system. I did not need a co-signer. My new home has all the features that I desire, including a spacious backyard and a playroom for my son. It has an upstairs, downstairs, and an unfinished basement which will be finished within the next few years. This time I didn't settle. I did my due diligence of saving money, improving my credit, researching, and waiting for the right opportunity. When the right door of opportunity opened for me, I walked through it with confidence expecting to obtain victory.

Chapter 5: Freedom Through Forgiveness

Last, but not least, I have committed to keep pushing forward and to not hold myself back by my past mistakes. I have chosen to free myself through forgiveness. Forgiving myself has allowed the healing process to flow freely. A healed heart is necessary for a productive and successful future. **Proverbs 4:23** states, "*Keep thy heart with all diligence; for out of it* ARE *the issues of life.*"

Chapter 6: My Story Continues

As long as I have breath in my body, I will continue to allow God to write my story. I have finally accepted that God has gifted me to do many things. I don't know why he has chosen me, but instead of wasting time feeling unworthy, I choose to make good use of the gifts that he has invested in me.

So, what's up next for Sherabim Joy? The answer is simple, perpetual triumph and continuous victories. I am committed to doing the things that bring joy to my soul. I will dream and pursue a balanced and healthy life for my son and me. I will write more books and minister to more souls. I will build a successful business and enjoy all the fruits of my labor. What won't I do? I won't settle. I deserve the best, and I am worthy of it, and I will keep pushing until my visions become manifested realities.

I must say that I am proud of myself. That is something

that I do not say enough. I am proud of Sherabim Joy Allen. Why? I am proud because I pushed past my quitting points, and I truly Triumphed. When was the last time that you told yourself what a great job you were doing? There are more than enough people in the world to criticize you; don't be one of them. Learn to acknowledge your failures but celebrate your success without regret.

May I encourage you? Whatever you do, please commit to not giving up. Triumph is closer to your reach than you think. Do whatever you need to do to be victorious. If you need help, please seek it. If you need to detach yourself from a toxic relationship, please do it expeditiously. You are created by a Victor to be victorious. Forgive yourself, and unapologetically allow your soul to triumph.

Meet Sherabim Joy

Sherabim Joy is an award-winning Christian author, preacher, motivational speaker, writing coach, and pastoral counselor based out of New Jersey. She is a powerful orator and has been a guest presenter at many revivals, conferences, empowerment sessions and universities.

She is also a prolific and creative writer providing messages of empowerment, as well as entertainment to her readers. She is the author of, two Christian novels "Mema's Pretty Little Black Girls" and Christian Indie award winning novel, "After the Benediction." Her non-fiction works "Heart of a Woman: Motherhood, Marriage, Ministry, and Money", and "Life Won't Wait", have blessed many lives. She is also the co-author of "A Mother's Love." Her first children's book entitled "Manny and the Magic Keys," was published in Summer 2020 and the second installment in the series will be published in the Spring/Summer of 2022.

Sherabim is a Certified Temperament Counselor and is trained and anointed to offer ministry counseling and support services to individuals expressing the need and/or desire for Biblical counseling using Temperament Therapy.

Sherabim is available for revivals, prayer services, empowerment sessions, seminars and workshops, coaching sessions, and counseling. To invite her to your next event or to inquire about other services please contact her email her at **soarwithsheri@gmail.com** or visit her website @: **WWW.SHERABIMJOY.COM**

My Monster Has a Name
Jessica Annice

I am a fat, Black woman with anxiety. It is a hellscape trifecta. Some people say that this can't be. That anxiety is not a Black people issue. "Girl, you better pray it away" is the adage. I am here to tell you it absolutely is a Black people issue. That an entire race could disown you for being transparent is enough to send a person into a panic. As I type this, I feel a heavy pain in the center of my chest.

As Black women, we are tasked with carrying the burdens of the entire race with poise and grace. We are the food. We are the life-givers. The light. We are fucking magic. We have to be perfect. There is no room for error. It is an impossible task.

Months before my diagnosis, I dealt with trauma after trauma. I was sexually assaulted, homeless, and unemployed. I couldn't see myself out of the darkness. The who, what, when, where, why, and how, of life left me broken. Once things started to settle and my life was moving in the right direction the monster had different plans and a new tactic. I had a record of twelve days without sleep, no naps, or catching a few winks here or there. My body and brain decided that I didn't need to sleep. I began to hallucinate and felt my organs giving up from lack of rest. I was losing my grip on life and reality. I was numb to the emotional toll the insomnia was taking on me. I didn't feel scared, sad, or even angry. I felt nothing.

In May 2017, I was diagnosed with a generalized anxiety disorder, which, in layman's terms, means I am a constant worrier. All day. Every single fucking day, my mind is constantly turning out thoughts of doom and dread. I worry about something I did fifteen years ago, fifteen days ago, fifteen minutes ago, and fifteen seconds of worrying about what I worried about. Consumed by imaginary scenarios of what my life will be like in an hour, or the next day, or the next year. It sounds foolish, but it's real. It's so fucking real. Intrusive thoughts on a constant replay in my mind.

In my experience, a severe storm rolls in suddenly, bringing palpitations, sweating, and chest pain. I hyperventilate, too. My vision becomes blurry, and everything that surrounds me disappears. Imagine a category five hurricane destroying your mind and ability to turn off your feelings, standing still, and bracing for the headwinds. The worst part is that I lose my ability to think clearly. It's like I can no longer trust my brain. Something isn't working right in there. I lost what it means to be human. To think. To feel. To breathe. To see. To be.

This is my experience with anxiety. Common symptoms include fatigue, sweating, restlessness, shortness of breath, a feeling of impending doom, insomnia, nausea, poor concentration, sensation of an abnormal heartbeat, or trembling, imagine a voice constantly telling you that your effort wasn't good enough. Questioning whether or not you completed your intended task. Do it over. You suck. Who, what, when, where, why, and how all damn day. It gets exhausting, but you can't sleep because you can't stop worrying. Insomnia is a cruel bitch. She attacks your tired body and feral mind like a ninja with a 70-inch serrated blade slowly slicing at your mind piece by piece. Hell of a description, huh? It's that brutal.

Anxiety, before I could put a name to it, caused me to sabotage significant opportunities in life, career, and love. I have walked away from so many amazing chances because of fear of not being good enough and ironically, too perfect. I have walked away from love because I felt that, eventually, they would get to know the real me and bail. I get comfortable enough to let my guard down, and that's when people become Olympic medalist-level runners. They bolt faster than Usain.

Career opportunities that could have changed my entire

life for the better, but I allowed fear to make me complacent. Stressing over imaginary scenarios caused me to be grossly unhappy. Fear has motivated my entire life. Fear of success. Fear of happiness.

I don't speak up when I need to be a powerful voice; I usually fade into the background and blend in the best I can. All the while, I think, "This isn't right. This is not okay. This is not who I am. I can't make too much noise because then I will be noticed. Then I will be the center of attention. I will be judged, poked, and prodded like cattle heading to slaughter." The monster mutes me.

"It's not that deep," people say. It's more than evident that I am harder on myself than anyone else could ever be. Here is the catch: I can't help it. This is not a choice. It's a lonely and frightening existence. I isolate myself to protect myself and the few relationships I have.

Slowly, I became my best friend, and anxiety is my greatest foe. Family and friends will always question, "Are you okay?" They will feel sorry for me for a while, sympathetic and helpful. Eventually, they will be afraid to be themselves around me. They watch what they say in my presence, presenting themselves as perfect examples of strong mental health and wondering if I am one trigger away from a freakout. Eventually, my "issues" always become too much, and I am left to battle with the monster.

Creating new bonds and relationships is damn near impossible because I always worry about what they think. I keep up walls as a defense because surely no one wanted to be friends with an overly anxious neurotic Black girl. Too many strikes. Too much drama. Just too fucking much.

Real and imaginary reactions cause me to retreat and not develop new relationships, causing me to be alone. Alone is where I feel safest, but I am not alone. The monster is always there, whispering devious thoughts in my ear.

My life is a perpetual state of trying and almost. "Trying" is a not-so-clever mechanism I developed to cope with failure over the years. Let me explain. Trying is my way to absolve the guilt of falling flat on my face. And this is in everyday tasks and relationships. Because even in "trying," it may not be my best effort, but I attempted to reach an intended or perceived goal. If it's a complete clusterfuck, I can say I tried. I could attempt it again or give up entirely without too much guilt, but it's never my best effort.

Oh, but that sneaky monster will slap me in the face and tell me that I will never be good enough. That is the only thing that is guaranteed. With anxiety, you are never truly alone.

Getting a confirmed diagnosis felt like I had an ally in this fight. It was devastating to hear that I was confirmed mentally ill, but I found peace in it, and I could exhale. I no longer shrink myself to keep my monster happy. I can navigate the uncertainty of my feelings by recognizing that I can't control everything. I avoid situations that are too loud and overstimulating. Anything that would cause me to have an attack is a no-go because I recognize my triggers.

They say dead women can't tell tales. I beg to differ. The Autumn Equinox is supposed to represent a time of reflection and harvest. It is a time to replenish your energy and store it for the winter. The cold days and darkness lie ahead but the harvest is a bright respite for days to come. September is always a tough month for me. My mother died in September. It is a month I associate with loss, death to be more specific. It represents a time of grief and deep sadness for me.

In September 2015, someone I considered a close friend, the closest thing I had to a brother, took something from me that

I could never get back. It was someone I talked to every single day for ten years. He knew about the monster and decided to join forces with it to destroy me. He knew everything there was to know about me and what made me Jessica. I trusted him as a friend, a confidant, a person I could depend on. He assaulted me on a cold Wednesday night in late September. He forced himself on me on my twice-passed-down couch while I wore my favorite sweater and most comfy socks.

On that dreary Wednesday evening, what he took wasn't my physical being or tangible. He butchered my sense of self. Who I was before he ended my life, as I have always known it, is just a mere memory. She is gone. I missed that girl. I missed her smile. She had a positive spirit. That girl had a purpose. She was full of hope. She had meaning. She had direction. That girl had a strong heartbeat. People always say that only you can control how you feel. But those people have never encountered a body snatcher, a soul thief, or a murderer. He took who I was and left behind a ghost. Over 400 showers couldn't resurrect me.

We sat on the couch, exchanged sentiment, "How are you?" kind of conversation, and shared a few inside jokes. He stood around six foot three, but he seemed larger than life that day. He teased me that I was dressed for a blizzard while sitting in my apartment. He grabbed me in an instant with the strength of what felt like ten men and forced my mouth open using his tongue. I will never forget he tasted like Starbucks. I was confused. Our friendship was completely platonic. There was no flirtation. I used to give him tips on how to get dates. We didn't talk about sexual things. We were friends. Why was this happening, I thought? I still ask myself what I did to cause this.

I screamed. I kicked. I punched. I tried to fight with every ounce of strength I had. I wasn't strong enough. The monster knew that I was too weak in mind and body to fight him off. That didn't stop me from trying to get him off me. He said no words just looked me in the eyes with this intense hate. His energy was black. The color of his eyes and even his touch were black. He is pure evil.

I saw him a few weeks after, crossing the street on Michigan Avenue against the light, dodging traffic. And my breath got caught in my lungs. I was trying to get away before he could see me, but my feet were concrete. Our eyes locked, and at that moment, I felt twenty-three stabs to my gut. Twenty-three for the number of times he thrust himself into me before he detonated. Twenty-three for the number of times he entered my womb without permission. Twenty-three times, he decided that my humanity didn't matter. All it took was twenty-three grunts to commit a murder. Twenty-three minutes left in that episode of "Amen" that played on the television while he assaulted me. In a haze of traffic, I perished once more. And many times, after that.

Every time I relive that day, it is a eulogy. A testament to who I once was. Here lies this sweet girl. A sister. A daughter. A niece. A cousin. A friend. She was born shortly after midnight in August 1983. She wanted to be a writer. Her life was cut tragically short because she decided to trust someone. She leaves behind an incomplete legacy because she has just begun to live. They say forgiveness helps people move on, but ghosts can't accept apologies.

After the assault, I lay on my couch in complete shock about what had happened to me. He used my underwear to clean himself off and left my apartment like nothing happened. Completely nonchalant. It is not like on the television shows. There are no compassionate detectives who approach you with empathy and support. I walked into the police station with hair messy, my shoes didn't match, and I was scared and completely anxious.

The monster was on my back, and I could do nothing to get rid of him as I relayed the incident to the police officers and handed them my underwear. I gave the officers all the information I had on the attacker from his phone number to his mother's home address. They promised to be in contact. I didn't feel brave or strong after I reported the crime. I didn't feel anything but dread and failure. What did I do to deserve this? It wasn't a stranger or someone in a back alley. This man was my friend and knew all my vulnerabilities. He knew when to strike, And I blamed myself for giving him the weapon.

I took a cab and went to the hospital, but I wanted to run back to the cab stand when I entered the chaotic emergency room. I remember feeling this wasn't important enough. People with real issues and illnesses needed help more. The monster and the newly formed alliance with my attacker had me in deep self-doubt. I felt violated again after the exam. They asked what felt like a million questions a minute. Sticking medcal instruments in every opening. It felt overly aggressive; I cried the entire time, and no one asked if I was okay. To say I felt less than human is an understatement. One ounce of compassion shown to me could have made all the difference in my mental state.

A few days later, I received a phone call from the police department informing me that they would not be pursuing charges. The monster laughed and gloated. Of course, no one would believe the fat girl could have been raped. I should have been lucky that someone even took the time to be my friend.

I lost everything after I knew that I would get no justice. I stopped taking care of myself. A few months after the assault, I was evicted from my apartment and went to live with my family. It was a rough go. I had all this fear and uncertainty inside and no one to talk to. I eventually ended up homeless again after a few months with my family. I slept in airport hotels, friend's couches, and even in the car at a Walmart parking lot on a few occasions. I moved from the state of Michigan and still did not escape. Running from my feelings only made matters worse. I lost so much more than my dignity. I was damaged goods from the inside out. I felt like everyone knew, although I had told no one but the police and the emergency room doctors.

I moved back to Michigan after realizing my friends weren't my healers or comfort. I needed to do the work myself. It was so hard realizing that I needed to get help. I was taught to keep it in and pray. My body began slowly failing. There were times I wouldn't get sleep for days. After a few months of being back in Michigan, I went to the hospital because I could not sleep for twelve days. I was hoping that they would admit me and give me the proper care. Once again, the lack of common compassion and bedside manners made me feel worse than what originally ailed me.

The scars from that night are permanently etched on my brain and body. It seemed like everyone knew I was damaged and blamed me for it. I didn't deserve to heal. I didn't see a doctor and a nurse practitioner prescribed me really strong antidepressants and sleeping pills. I never filled the script. I didn't want to fall into a stupor where I would forget what happened. I didn't want to be blinded or under any influence. I needed to confront the monsters in my life head-on, and I couldn't do that if I wasn't sober.

I wasn't a warrior. I'm a hopeless romantic, head in the clouds, happy-go-lucky person. But these foreign bodies that attached themselves to me tried to erase the innocence I once used to view the world. My rose-colored glasses took on a Black tint. I didn't want to become cynical and hard. I understood that I had to tap into a version of myself that I didn't know existed. For years after the assault, I was controlled by the experience and how his hands touched me without permission. I fought and did everything they said to do in the situation, but it still happened, and he still got away with it.

Getting my life back on track was one of the hardest things I ever had to do. The hardest part was doing it alone. The monster convinced me that no one would care. Why should they care about what happened to me? The monster said I should have fought harder, screamed louder, bit him, punched him. For a very long time,, I thought the monster was right, but I couldn't continue to live tormented. Not sleeping or eating and letting the few relationships I had deteriorate. The monster and my attacker could not succeed in completely isolating and destroying me. I had to do something.

I found a sexual assault support group and an amazing therapist who listened to me. Respected that I didn't want to live a life just floating along trying not to remember what happened to me. Talk therapy saved my life. I do not want to forget what happened to me. I want to feel safe and not flinch when people touch me. I want to be affirmed without thinking if a person has an ulterior motive. I want to feel worthy of love and romance. Healing isn't linear, it is constant. It has been years, and I still feel the shame behind this now and again. I live a few miles from where my attacker lives. I saw him cutting his lawn once, and once again, I felt those sharp pains in my groin and his rough hands groping my body. All over again, I felt the weight of his six-foot-three frame holding me down with brute force. I felt the pain of trying my hardest to fight him off with no success. My mind would take me back to that fall day and I would become paralyzed with fear. I would feel dirty, and all the shame would come rushing back.

Living a life enshrined in fear is a thing of the past. While this monster is a lifelong companion, I have no longer chosen to make it an enemy. I will embrace the chaos because I know this is not my fault. I won't hide behind the monster any longer and face my fears head-on. Believe me, that is more challenging than it seems. I have moments where I fear what it means to take a step. The feeling that the world will crumble beneath me. In those moments, I use my diagnosis as a platform to elevate myself out of the hypnosis of self-doubt. My life is not defined by my association with the monster and its influence on my life; instead, it is by how I prevail and triumph during the uncertainty of it. There is always another minute or another moment to be better. To do better.

My battles with the monster have made me stronger than I ever imagined. Healing is a lifelong journey. I have my necessary weapons of mindfulness and being aware of keeping me from falling into the monster's web. I can only control myself and my reactions. On this healing journey, I know I am the only person. I am not responsible for anyone's thinking but my own. I am taking the necessary steps to combat the intrusive thoughts at the first feeling of doubt and fear. There is peace in being still. In those moments, we find clarity. The defenses I built over the years are now used to fight the monster. I am no longer battling with my thoughts. I know my enemy, and I will not be defeated.

Meet Jessica Annice

Jessica Annice is an aspiring author whose love for writing is only second to her love of reading. Born and raised in Detroit, MI., Jessica uses her love for the city and advocacy for mental health as a foundation for her writing. She believes that words heal.

Her stories and experiences strive to make people feel seen and heard in spaces they would otherwise be ignored. When she is not reading or penning a story, she is a couch internet sleuth watching true crime shows.

Currently, Jessica Annice has three stories on Amazon's episodic stories KindleVella platform. Connect with Jessica Annice on Instagram @futurebstseller.

Out of the Ashes
Lacha J. Barnes

To live or die was the only decision that I needed to make. Years of ups and downs, apologies, empty promises and even more. The drama never ceased to end within my marriage. Even when I forgave and decided to stay, internally there was no fulfilment or satisfaction. Memories of the day we said, "I do," flooded my mind.

All of the time I spent seeking a ring and a marriage to last forever, my self-esteem took hit after hit. After a bad car accident that was designed to take my life as well as my unborn child's, I gave my life to Christ. Once I delivered my second daughter, I issued an ultimatum. Marry me or I take these precious babies of ours and we are leaving. Finally, August 29, 1994, he and I stood in the courthouse filling out the application for our marriage license.

Little did I know that the defeated look on my children's father's face and the words spoken to his mother pertaining to marriage being a ball and chain situation, would be foretelling of what was to come. When I look back over my life, I shudder at all the bad choices I made, the many years I suffered as well as settled for a piece of man. Barely two months into our marriage, my children's father stopped coming home at night. Constantly he lied about his whereabouts so that I would not suspect that he was cheating.

Abuse ran rampant in our home because I never learned how to just let things be. I was not the kind of woman who would sit back and ride. When I think about things now, my talking back and raising hell did not make me strong. Nor did it look like I would take my life into my hands and get my girls and myself out of the matrix my life had become. Instead of peace, love joy, and happiness being my portion, I wore a garment of sadness, anxiety, chronic depression, and unhealthy eating. Sleepless nights, verbal arguments, emotional and mental abuse became my normal.

My youngest baby loved her father outwardly. What I mean is that she was the peacekeeper of the two girls. She did not like to see her father and me argue or see me crying. When my baby girl watched days turn into nights and her father had not come home, she would call his cell phone relentlessly. Each time the voicemail picked up, she left messages for him to come home and that she loved him oh so much. She hardly slept, like me. She would lie awake late into the midnight hour trying to wait up for him to come home, but that did not happen most times. My oldest was introverted as it pertained to how she felt about family life. She was a girl of few words. She never shared what was on her mind or heart.

I was always upset about something. Mad at God for not making my then- husband honor me; and love me enough not have girlfriends on the side. In my ignorance, I had more than one Job moment when he questioned God about why all the things that were happening in his life. He reminded God of how he was faithful, prayed for forgiveness on behalf of his children, and was a righteous man who loved the Lord. I could not fathom why God would not fix him. I felt as if God left me to myself, and I handled things in a way that I am ashamed of today. My heart was hurting, and my spirit was crushed. I loved going to church, but I thought I would punish God for not giving me my husband back. Giving my girls their father back so that we could raise them together.

While I watched every televangelist that came on television, read God's Word, and listened to His Music, nothing could soothe my fatigue and emptiness. My children's father would come home every few days; he missed birthdays, and some holidays because he was out with his side piece. I hounded him every time he hit the door. Questions I expected answers from him were, "Where have you been," "Who were you with," "Why don't you answer your phone when I call you," and 'Why don't you return my calls when you get the voicemails?" He perfected the art of dodging the fiery darts thrown his way, deflecting, and then turning the situation around and making me out to be the guilty party. It was all he needed to go right back out the door into the arms of another woman.

The girls were usually in earshot and heard many of our arguments. Surprisingly, they never asked me why Daddy left. I lacked the wisdom to know that what my daughters were privy to and would one day bite me in the behind. They were all I had. I vented to them. I cried and we would all pray for Daddy to come home. Never once did I think that my actions would be of disservice to them later in life. No one taught me how to deal with marital issues or protect the children's safety by keeping them away from our dysfunction and problems. I was a newly saved wreck who used the Bible as a whooping book full of judgments and self-righteous behavior.

Fooling myself, I thought I wanted the truth of why my life was in shambles and tried to convince anyone who would listen that I could handle the truth. I knew the truth; I just needed to hear him say it. The phone calls started coming into my home and each time I felt as if I had been slapped in the face and once in front of my daughter. The magnitude of the disrespect was more than I could bear on many occasions. I was blown away by his side pieces boldness.

After they got over their surprise of a wife answering, they called for him as if it were the most natural thing in the world. They loved to call me when he was with them, telling me about how my ex-husband did not want to be with me because I did not make him feel like they did. I guess the old saying is true; someone is waiting in the wings to do what your girl will not do. I cried so much during those sixteen years. I cursed, broke stuff, and thought several times about taking him out when he was home. Anger, jealousy, and murder stayed on my mind. Being nice got old, and being upset made no difference to him.

Only those who have lived through infidelity in their marriage can understand the havoc the enemy plays on the mind. I would stay awake late at night looking at the empty side of the bed knowing that he was with someone else. I would get down on my knees and cry and pray to God about bringing my ex-husband home. It did not dawn on me then that I was still missing the point that I needed God to fix what was broken inside of me that caused him to be unfulfilled. The minutes turned into hours and finally the new day would dawn. I remembered going outside at the break of dawn one morning. I looked up and down the driveway, crying because I saw black vultures or black birds circling around our parking lot. I believed that when black vultures flew around, someone had died. I thought something happened to him.

Nothing I did made a difference. I went from loving my husband to hating him from minute to minute. The days were extremely long. Depression visited me just as it had done most of my teen years. I was hopelessly in love with a man who loved me in his way which, that did not possess the qualities necessary to address my needs beyond the bedroom. One night after I returned from my first cruise with my cousin, my phone rang at eleven-thirty. The caller- Id showed a number I recognized right off. Before that night, I would see this phone number on the pager and on the first cell phone I purchased for him. Upon picking up the phone, the female introduced herself and was telling me all the things my ex-husband had shared with her. She made sure to let me know that he didn't love me, but she also confessed that he led her on and how she was not interested in being with someone else's husband. By the time the call ended, anxiety showed up and had taken over.

Ignorance will keep you entangled in situationships, and relationships until you begin to look at things with a different mindset and eye. Due to a lack of theological education, I gave my husband more than I gave to God, worshipping the man, who left me broken. I should have been seeking God on changing things in me that could have been pushing him away. I wanted God to make him stop doing what he was doing with who he was doing it with, but that happened years later. A child was born, a boy that I desired to have, but I had all girls. "Why God?" I asked time after time. Why was he blessed to have what I was not granted to the grace with this other woman. When I found out about his illegitimate baby, I tried my best to beat the brakes off him.

Angry again with God, the struggle to understanding why I was cursed. Why when I pleaded for a boy each time I was pregnant, why did I only have girls? Disgust and bitterness began to creep up into my heart. Believe me when I say this. Thinking, overthinking, what was it all about? I never wondered what would happen if I continued to stay in a relationship with the man I pledged my love and faithfulness to for the remainder of my days. I could not make heads or tails of what God was doing and how He would get the glory from the mess I called my life.

In Two thousand three, while I travailed amid the storms of my relationship, Breast Cancer visited me. Not once but twice. I did not believe that God loved me, surely I had been a horrible person. My past was sketchy at best and one day I will tell that story. How could a loving God, whom I served despite my marriage being in shambles, allow me to have to endure anything more? My children's father came home long enough to take me to procedures, treatments, and testing back home again. He would still leave the girls home with me. My youngest could not articulate her fears of the possibility of her mommy dying. She picked up anger and treated me like I was the enemy. I cried many days, nights, feeling defeated, and worthless. My oldest daughter did not lash out in anger, she became withdrawn.

I recall the time in two thousand four, I had tram flap

reconstruction surgery. I underwent a mastectomy two weeks prior. My six -hour surgery turned into an all- day affair. My mother's nerves were on end as she waited at home all day for someone to call and let her know how things went. Things were a blur and once I came from recovery to my room heavily sedated, I could hear her fussing about why no one called her. She told me I was just getting out of surgery. After putting her eyes on me, she left. My pastor came in long enough to see that I was still breathing, kissed my cheek, and I slept until mid-morning the next day.

After my release a week later, nothing changed at home. My children became my caretakers at ages nine and eleven. My ex-husband returned to his other life as if I had not spent a week in the hospital after having one of the most serious surgeries I had ever experienced. Not long after getting home, I had a coughing spell that would not stop. I was afraid for my life as I was stapled from hip to hip. Bursting my stomach frightened me as well as my girls. With no one to call, I had my oldest call my pastor. My baby asked her to pray for me.

Those next months of treatments, sickness, fatigue, and healing were nearly impossible to endure. The only thing that helped me move through days in a blur was the prescriptions of Vicodin. I took them to numb the pain and help me sleep through the nights that were otherwise unbearable. I found my laugh again and kept my girls close just in case. By September of the same year, I had been diagnosed with metastatic Herceptin receptor positive malignant Breast Cancer and more chemotherapy treatments to follow. One morning as I got my babies up for school, my youngest could barely walk straight and for the first time I realized that she had lost weight dramatically. A few days later, I took her for testing, and she was diagnosed with Hodgkins Lymphoma stage three B.

That started another whirlwind of traumatic experiences I would endure. My daughter's illness brought their father home.

My daughter was admitted to the children's hospital and by that time, she had lost sight in one eye, and her ability to stand was waning. The tumor was too large to remove from her chest without crushing her organs and she coded twice. Prayers were solicited all around the city. Here we go again, were my thoughts. Was I not humble enough? I just could not wrap my head around the whirlwind that had become my life. My baby girl and I were like Siamese twins, joined at the hip. Once told the diagnosis, her last words for almost a month, were, "Mommy, am I going to die?"

My children's father stayed home to care for our oldest daughter who was only twelve years old. She used her cell phone as a way of escape, her fears were locked behind the walls of her mind. Arguments and disagreements were happening at home while my baby fought for her life in the pediatric intensive care unit of Duke Children's Hospital. Our family was brought back together through this storm or so it seemed. My battle brought my family back together, even if on and off. By the grace of God, my daughter survived and beat Hodgkins Lymphoma. I had to fight longer and harder, but God caused me to prevail.

There were times I wavered in my convictions of right and wrong as they pertained to my marriage. Detached, I went through the motions of life day in and day out until I met up with one of my classmates I had not seen in over fifteen years. He and I began to talk. It was nothing meaningful at first, but as time moved forward an emotional tie was born. Loneliness was no longer an issue, and anxiety had taken a back seat as I felt alive again. Initially I struggled with my convictions of right and wrong, but it was already too late. When I should have been saying no to meetups and telephone conversations, I did the opposite and crossed lines that I never should have.

In my mind, I was on my way to getting a divorce from my children's father. A few months later, I told him of I had been unfaithful. His heart was crushed. He had been broken down, taken off the mountain of falsities. Before that time, I had never been unfaithful to him, or should I say in moments of honesty I never acted upon any thought I had. He consistently told me that he never thought I would step out on him, anyone but me. I emphasized that I didn't do anything to get back at him, but I was cold to him. There was no interest in being with him any longer, and my plans were to leave. Seeing him day in and day out dragging around, hurting caused me grief. Unfortunately, the mental and emotional abuse he caused me did not have the same effect on him.

Failing God was my biggest regret. Conviction turned into guilt, and I know that the Word of God says that now there is no condemnation to those who are in Christ Jesus and walk not after the flesh but after the spirit. I met with my pastor and bore my soul to her. She knew what I had been living with for over eleven years. More than anything, she was concerned about my soul. Had I repented she wanted to know. I confirmed that I had as well as cut off the relationship with my friend. We both walked in fully aware of my situation, however I felt it necessary to apologize to him. Ending what were only ever to be fleeting moments of comfort was not easy, but necessary. Many years later, I still am in disbelief that I did this. I hurt my relationship with God, my kids' father, and myself.

Journaling and forgiveness kept me going. My children didn't know what I had done until years later when I told them. We never missed a beat during that season of my life. I was home with them, and I had never confessed my indiscretion, no one would have known but God, the individual and I. My conscience would not allow me to remain quiet as it pertained to my daughters. God did not ordain my union with my ex-husband. In my naiveté at twenty-three years of age, I fell in lust and then love. Our relationship was toxic from day one. Not all days were bad days; however, there were more bad days or not-so-good days, than great days. It took years for me to understand that love does not hurt. That love is kind, gentle, knows no wrong, and so many other things. My indiscretion brought him home for good. Filled with hope, I decided to stay. and after fifteen years of marriage, he proposed after sharing his indiscretions in front of the whole church. My heart was conflicted because the residue of all that had transpired in our relationship was stubborn like a stain. While I continued to seek the forgiveness of God, I also prayed to fall in love with my ex-husband again. Shock cloaked my face as he shared his heart with the congregation. His sin was visible to everyone since there was no shame while he was living a double life. Many knew about it, and although they did not express their feelings to me, I am sure they silently questioned why I stayed.

On bended knee, he stood before me. I can- not remember the exact words, but he proposed. He had not done so when we first got married, but he had finally decided that he did not want to lose his family. Pictures of our past flashed through my mind as I stood there. I remained quiet, time escaped me. Happiness and sadness ran through me at the same time. Questions of why now, how come it took fifteen years of my heartache, embarrassment, feelings of less than, and our children's heartbreak and abandonment for him to choose us finally. I said yes because I did not want to embarrass him while he bent on one knee, presenting me with a new ring. The church cried, congratulated, had all the men saluting him.

At the end of the day, I just wanted to be happy. It still had not dawned on me that I would never be his number- one lady. The disclaimer I gave to him before our vow renewal was that I would not be unhappy for the next five years. The day I walked down the aisle, my day was made because my daddy walked with me. He never knew all that I endured with his son-in-law. I did not want my father to worry about me, nor did I want him to try and force me to leave. Although we stood at the altar and spoke our vows as well as reminisced on some good times, it proved not to be enough.

Twenty-one years later, I had finally taken all I was going

to take. After my book signing, I informed my children's father that I wanted a divorce. I went on to advise him that I wasn't looking for change or for him to do anything different; I just wanted out. I walked away from one of the worst relationships I had ever been in. Leaving everything behind, it was time for me to start over. Tired of trying and torn down in my mental, emotional state, I said no more. It was the darkest time of my life. I was three years into my pastoral ministry, I felt like a failure. How could I manage God's house when I couldn't manage my own home where my first ministry lived. Why would anyone listen to a word I spoke? How could I convince two to remain married when I had left my marriage and home? Why did I stay longer than I should have? Why is it my grown children are now seeking love in the wrong places? Why is it that our relationship went from we were all we had to blaming me for staying? How do I right the wrongs of yesterday gone by?

In the dark place trying to consume me, I went back to my home church and refused to give up on the work God had ordained for me to do. I still cried night after night, but never in front of my girls. Depression and anxiety had come back and made themselves comfortable in my psyche. Many days I did not want to get up and go to work, church or out of the house. Turmoil and division swirling were around my family, and at times I felt powerless despite knowing a God who cannot fail. I am grateful for the prayers of my pastor and others who loved me beyond the season I was in.

Slowly the heaviness that I wore day after day out began to lift, and I could finally breathe again. The adversary tried to keep me in solitude while he launched an assault on my spiritual health. Some days I had nothing but time and questioned myself why. Why had I wasted time renewing vows only to end up here? That was the last chance I gave to my kids' father and our marriage. Walking away was one of the hardest things to do. At times I believed it would be the end of me, but someone was praying for me. Those who have been married and have experienced infidelity, abuse, and longsuffering can relate to what I was going through.

God had delivered me from the hand of the enemy time and time again. This time would be no different. He knew that I would never be fulfilled in my marriage because my ex-husband could not love me or treat me the way I desired and needed. Certainly, I did not want to live the rest of my life alone, but at the same time, I felt it was what I deserved. Who walks away after twenty-one years of marriage and twenty-five years of relationship?

God knows what you need and is a promise keeper. His Word says, if you delight yourself in me, I will give you the desires of your heart. Seek ye first the kingdom of God and His righteousness and all things will be added unto you. I got busy again in kingdom building and rededicating my life to the work of the His ministry. When the opportunity came to love again I ran in the other direction. I supervised my current husband at work. We were friends first and he loves the Lord. He would ask me out and I would decline due to work ethics. He stayed the course and asked if he could court me. In front of my family, he proposed to me on my birthday the following year. I made sure to tell him about everything from my previous marriage. There was no judgement detected in his face or eyes when I searched them. He promised to catch me if I fell, and he has been doing just that since then.

A year and a half later, we were married and recently celebrated five years of marriage. We work together in ministry after relocating to another state. He supports me in everything that I do from being present, encouraging me, leading, praying for, and covering me. My marriage today looks nothing like the past and I am grateful to say that I am abundantly blessed. The places God can take you when you are a willing participant. Marriage is work, but I am thankful that I am working with him and not alone. I remember God's word where He said that he did not refine us as with silver, but in the furnace of affliction. My praise brings Him glory as He works to sanctify me even more as I do the work that secures my eternity. When God birthed beauty out of my ashes.

Meet Pastor Lacha J. Barnes

Pastor Lacha' Barnes is a multi-faceted vessel of God. She is the Executive Pastor serving at Kingdom Covenant Empowerment Center in Dinwiddie, Va.

Pastor Lacha' is the wife of Jemonis Barnes, mother of three daughters, grandmother of two grandsons and one granddaughter. Pastor Lacha' is a published author of Speak of the Devil & Up Pops the Devil, playwright of "Now I Believe, "Grace Restored," preacher and teacher of the unadulterated Gospel of Jesus Christ.

Pastor Lacha' sits on the board of Kingdom Covenant International Fellowship as the International General Administrator, holds a master's degree in Christian Education and is the visionary of God's Girls Rock NC-Va, which is a teen mentorship for God's leading ladies.

Lacha' understands the need for continual prayer and interceding on behalf of those in need as she is a survivor of recurrent metastatic Breast Cancer. Her favorite scripture is Romans 8:28; For we know all things work together for the good of those who love the Lord and are called according to His purpose.

Dancing in the Rain With a Purpose
Stories Behind the Smile
Dr. Annie R. McClain

"Then the word of the Lord came unto me, saying before I formed you in the belly, I knew thee, and before you camest forth out of the womb, I sanctified thee. And I ordained thee a prophet unto the nations."
Jeremiah 1:45

Traveling Pedophile

I was adopted at eight months old and introduced to the power of prayer early in life. Our spiritual beliefs were grounded in the Apostolic Doctrine.

One afternoon my mother and I were shelling peas and out of the blue, she told me that God gifted me to do great work for Him, an assignment only I could do. She said *I was that person who would always be available to help others.* But I didn't understand at the time what she was saying. I was only eleven years old, and I wasn't concerned about what God wanted me to do. His purpose for my life was the last thing on my mind. Of course, I was taught that He created everything for a reason and a specific purpose, but having an assignment from Him only I could fulfill wasn't registering with me. As far as I was concerned, it was a pointless conversation.

Growing up without siblings was difficult. I didn't have a big sister or big brother to mimic. No one was there to help me understand how to survive in my environment from a child's point of view. Additionally, I couldn't play away from home with other children my age. So, I never had the opportunity to gain experience of how people formed their thoughts about others or how to protect myself from human prey. As I grew older, I became sickly. At 8, I had pneumonia, a boil behind my right knee when I was ten, and several other minor illnesses. At thirteen, I developed migraine headaches.

At times, the headaches were so brutal, I just wanted to die. From that point forward, my life was like a box of chocolates; I never knew which piece I would eat from one day to the next. It was one upheaval after the other. Playing the card game of life forced me to learn how to dance in the rain. But at the end of the day, playing the game worked in my favor. I didn't have a choice! Although I kept smiling, my heart was broken and shattered into tiny pieces, and no one knew. Emotionally, I was a wreck! I didn't believe I had the strength to endure what it would take to put my heart back together again. So, at thirteen, I was willing to give up and call it quits by any means necessary. *Many times, I thought about taking the easy way out.*

My health continued to decline. The headaches got so bad I lost vision in my right eye. My mother tried every remedy she could find trying to relieve the headaches, but to no avail. Dr. Purnell was the only physician in the city. On the recommendation of a close friend, mom arranged a visit with him. He said because my hair was so long it was causing tension headaches, and he suggested that Mom should cut my hair. I loved my hair! It was exceptionally long, thick black curls hanging just below my waist. I immediately got upset and stormed out of his office. But she didn't cut it. Instead, she took me to a tent meeting to see a healer.

They called him the Traveling Elder, (*I call him the demon*) a preacher who came through our town every year, preaching under a tent in the Branch Section. He claimed to be a healer. One night, he called for the sick to come up for prayer and healing. Of course, Mom took me to the altar. She explained my condition and asked if he could heal me. He immediately took out a bottle, poured something into his hand, and began to rub my head, running his hands through my hair and caressing my scalp. I precipitously got sick to my stomach. I couldn't look at him when he finished his healing ritual, praying in a different language and rubbing my head.

Back in the day, growing up, my parents didn't talk much about love. If they fed you, kept a roof over your head, clothed you, and kept you safe, that's how they expressed their love for you. A hug or a kiss just because or before leaving the house was out of the question. Instead, a little wink, pinch on the cheek, or going to the store and buying your favorite ice cream cone was how they expressed their love.

If unique circumstances or an emergency occurred, I would stay with a family member, friend, or neighbor. I can't recall ever hearing my parents discuss my physical, emotional, or sexual safety when they placed me in the care of a trusted friend. *Sexually molesting* a child didn't seem to be a concern. ***But*** it should have been the *number one* concern. Instead, mutual trust between family members, *clergy,* and neighbors was evident.

On my fourteen birthday I passed out, and my parents took me to the emergency room. When I awakened, the Traveling Elder was in the room. He and my parents were conversing with the doctor. He told the doctor that he practiced faith and natural healing, and that he had prayed and anointed my head before, and the headaches ceased. A lump gathered in my throat, and I couldn't breathe. I was gasping for breath and banging my hands on the railings, trying to dispute what he was sharing with him. My actions resulted in the *demon* looking back at me with the coldest, darkest eyes I had ever seen. Then the doctor directed his question to my mother. I suppose he was confused over the immediate offer from the demon to perform a healing ritual to rid me of the migraines. He asked my mom if it was true about my headaches. Mom looked back at me and asked if my head had been hurting? I broke down because I knew what was coming next.

It was commonplace for a traveling preacher to stay at a church member's home. The Traveling Elder wasn't preaching in a church; he was a tent preacher. My adopted parents revered preachers, missionaries, bishops, and elders. In fact, anyone that said they had been called into the ministry, my parents gave them the utmost respect. *For this reason*, The demon was given a place in our home until the tent revival was complete. That was the day the trajectory of my life changed forever. I remember that day graphically, as if it were just yesterday.

Every June, he came to our town wearing a long black overcoat, a brown pouch across his shoulders, and his long silky salt and pepper hair was loose and free about his shoulders. The Traveling Elder was Native American with an awe-inspiring voice, almost hypnotic. My parents seemed enthralled by him, but something about him caused a knot to find a home in the pit of my stomach.

It was three weeks of going to the tent revival. The demon touched my head and massaged my scalp every night during his proclaimed healing ritual. My body automatically went into spazzing mode; involuntarily shaking, sweaty palms, pounding headache. *It was a horrible experience!* One night during the performance, his touch disturbed my psyche so intensely, that my knees weakened, and I slowly slid to the ground. I guess he thought I had received the *Holy Ghost*. When he reached to help me up, I screamed for help. My entire body was shaking; breathing was sporadic; I couldn't stand steady on my feet; the sound of a lion rang out so loud inside the tent. Fear rose, and I ran out toward my friend's house. The following day I finally understood what had happened. I was embarrassed for myself and my mother. My adopted dad didn't usually attend the tent meetings. I really don't believe he cared that much for the Traveling Elder, but for my mom's sake, he didn't object to him being around. The meeting ended that Friday night. I was happy as could be because the demon would leave our house. But he didn't leave! I was devastated!

He seems to always choose a chair directly across from me at the dinner table. He knew that was aggravating, but he got a kick out of sitting across from me with his evil eyes, piercing and cold, frowns stitched across his brow; I could feel his eyes scanning my body, undressing me. I wanted to choke the life out of him. One evening he got up from his chair, walked over to me, standing with one hand in his pocket, and put his other hand on my head. My body stiffened, and cold shivers took over. I wanted to run, but run where?

"How is your head today, Anne?" while running his hands through my long curly hair. My stomach was bubbling with anxiety, and the air accumulating inside didn't leave much room for food. So, I asked Mom if I could go to my room. As I left the table, he reached out, caught my hand, and began praying, telling God to keep me safe from evil things, men, women, and children. He took a bottle from his pocket, poured a red liquid into his hand, and started rubbing my head and running his hands through my hair again. He was squeezing my hand so tight I couldn't pull free. He stood up, still holding my hand tightly, and continued praying aloud. I couldn't understand what he said. He was speaking in another language. I was so scared that I wet my pants. *That's what set me free, wetting my pants.*

Embarrassed and shaking, I ran to my mother's room, calling out to her. Mom came behind me, sat on the, pulled me close to her side, and asked what was wrong with me. *What's wrong? Don't you see what's about to happen*? That's what was floating around in my head. *The demon! The evil one! That's what's wrong.* I couldn't eat anything that evening, and I didn't feel sick, but I was vomiting all over everything. I couldn't stop! Can you imagine a fourteen-year-old wetting her pants? That was humiliating! I couldn't look Mom in the face. She sat with me close to her side, putting cold towels on my throat and rubbing my stomach. Finally, the vomiting stopped, and I calmed down. Mom was holding my head when the Traveling Elder and Dad entered the room. He reminded my parents that he had healing hands, and God told him to anoint me. He said that God told him to start at my head and move to the bottom of my feet, which would heal me from the headaches. He said his work was of God, and God answered his prayers. Mom gasped and said no! With a god-awful look and frowning at my mom, he asked intensely if they wanted him to get rid of my headaches? They both resoundingly said yes! So, they agreed to let him pray and anoint me with oil. He then asked Mom and Dad to give him privacy because he needed to talk with God about my condition.

I knew in my heart that this shouldn't happen. How could I stop it? I didn't have a way out. I couldn't do anything to shield myself from this monster! I didn't know how to pray like my parents, but I had to do something. With tears streaming down my face, I began to pray in my head. *God, I need you. Please come and rescue me right now!* I remembered the bible verse we were required to learn in Sunday School; "*Jehovah is my shepherd, I shall not want. He makes me lie down in green pastures. He leadeth me beside still waters; he restoreth my soul; he leadeth me in the path of righteousness for his name's sake. Yay, though I walk through the valley of the shadow of death, I will fear no evil for thou are with me ....*" (Psalm 23). *Are you here, God? Are you with me? Can you hear me? I have been left alone with pure evil itself.*" I need you to rescue me, *Jesus!*"

The *demon* sat on the edge of my bed, staring in my eyes. Looking into his eyes was like looking into a black hole. He didn't have a soul! I didn't see anything but darkness. Finally, I yelled out, and he clamped his hand over my mouth. Then, squeezing my cheeks with his thumb on my nose, he said quietly, "*Shut up!*" He held my cheeks tightly until I shook my head, indicating I would be quiet. Then he said, "*I am not going to hurt you; I am going to make you feel good.*

I started to cry. So many thoughts were running around in my head. I thought he was trying to hypnotize my soul with his dark, cold, lifeless eyes. Why was I feeling this way? I don't know. But I knew he was trying to do something to me through his eyes. My fear of the Traveling Elder grew stronger and stronger by the minute. Squeezing my arm, with an angry look covering his face, he said, "I could take you away from your parents, and it would be easy because they trust me." I can't begin to explain how petrified that comment resonated with me, because he was telling the truth, they did trust him.

Although my parents stood outside the door, I felt helpless and alone. In my confused fourteen years-old mind, I'm screaming for help, and no one is coming to my rescue; no one hears me. Can't they see the fear in my eyes? How can they not see what this evil demon is doing to me? I would rather die than have his hands all over me. Our Apostolic faith taught against suicide; you would be taking something you couldn't give back and you would burn in hell. But that day, death would have been the least of the two evils.

Suddenly, he left the room; I was unsure of what happened or why he left so suddenly. Then, I heard he and my parents talking outside the doorway, "I will be back tomorrow with my healing oils and anoint her to help drive the spirit of sickness away." Mother and Dad agreed. How can they let him do this to me? Why will they allow this devil to violate my body? His hands will be all over me! In the eyes of the believers, men of the cloth were extraordinary. They believed that God sent them. They thought that they were his prophets and could do no wrong. *This is an age-old misconception!* Some men and women of the cloth are pure evil!

As the evening progressed, the vomiting started back. Finally, late that night, I ate some chicken broth and saltine crackers. Emotionally I was calm, not crying, and my chest wasn't tight. But as we were preparing for bed, there was a loud knock at the door; the Traveling Elder returned. I thought he was gone for the night, but I forgot that it was our house where he would stay while in town. Mom told me I would sleep on a pallet in her and Dad's room. I was so happy about that. That was the first full night's sleep I could remember since the demon had been in our home.

It was Saturday, and Mom always allowed me to sleep in on Saturday. The sun shining through the window was stimulating. I felt much better than the day before. I jumped up from the pallet, running through the house to the kitchen, still in my nightgown. I had forgotten the Traveling Elder had stayed over the night before. So, who was sitting at the table with Mom drinking coffee? The monster! Cold chills engulfed me like a rushing wind. My stomach tightened, and my heart wanted to leap from my chest. I froze!

And yes, anointing my body with healing oils happened. My mother stayed in the room while this humiliating, degrading, sexual molesting act occurred. Did it matter to him that she remained in the room? He still massaged my buttocks and tried to get me to turn over so he could "anoint" my chest, but I refused. I was molested while my mother stood by. That was the day my world stopped. He violated my body in plain sight! I remember how sick I felt, so cold and afraid, sweaty palms, and my heart was racing a thousand miles per minute. Feelings of betrayal, shame, and loneliness were so intense that I passed out again.

The last thing I remembered was asking God to let me die right then and there! *You said you know my name and that I am yours, so let me come home to you! Please don't wait a minute longer.* I woke up in my mother's bed with a cold towel on my forehead. When I was fully responsive, she asked, *"If I had been reading my bible. How do you know a verse from the book of Isaiah? You were talking aloud, telling God that he said he knew your name and that you wanted to come to live with Him."*

"I don't know, Mom," sharply. I was agitated with her. She looked at me strangely and continued rubbing my head. With her right hand over my heart, she began to pray. She asked God to forgive her for what she had allowed to happen. Tears rested on her cheeks. She kissed me and smiled. I didn't know what to do

or say to her. So, I went to sleep with my head resting on her shoulders and her hand over my heart.

The lingering trauma I encountered from the rubdown was emotionally and mentally draining. It made me feel like a nobody, a piece of trash, a whore! I saw myself as damaged goods at fourteen years old. To know that a fake man of God molested me in front of my mother was unbearable. I couldn't look her in the eyes most of the time. So, I climbed inside the dark hole I created for myself and lived there for *three months; mute, a silent child* for three months. I didn't choose this coping behavior because I could; it was essential for my survival. Being silent was my life support.

All I ever wanted in life was to be a good woman. And if God said so, I wanted to be the wife he described in *Proverbs 18:22.* I wanted to be an empathetic, caring, and nurturing wife who was precious in God's and her husband's eyes. But unfortunately, at fourteen-years-old, I was diagnosed with situational anxiety and depression, and an adjustment disorder. As a result, I lost all hope of a career assisting at-risk individuals. Being a victim of molestation almost sucked the life out of me. It forced me to give up on God, myself, and the possibility of becoming a wife and a mother. My dream of helping the misfortunate and brokenhearted had been destroyed. I would be lucky if I lived to see my fifteenth birthday.

Fear Was My Nemesis

Eighteen years old, a senior in school, and five years since the molestation. I was broken and bruised on the inside. But I managed to keep a smile on my face. Nightmares and anxiety attacks continued to haunt me. And preparing for graduation triggered the frequency of attacks. Not being consistent with attending school made it difficult to graduate. Although I was academically astute, sitting for nine exams and earnig ninety or above to pass two subjects was scary. The urge to drop out of school or do bodily harm was very tempting.

I stopped eating again and went on lockdown. I was afraid to go out because my fear was triggered by what I thought people would say. Proverbs 29: 25 says, "The fear of others traps people..." At that time (and sometimes now as an adult), I worked hard to overcome other people's opinions about me. And the feelings of shame and a lack of self-worth crowded the frontal lobe of my brain. I tried desperately to be normal, but my intense dislike for the people who hurt me became my second skin. As a result, my energy level was low and almost stagnant, and my mental health was in danger.

Attending school wasn't good for me. It was my hell on earth. I believed everyone at my school knew I was damaged. Some of my classmates would leave nasty notes on my desk; they made fun of me and called me odious names. My nicknames were *attention seeking freaking bitch and a suicidal whore*. Those words tore me to pieces on the inside. Once during an assembly, someone put a wad of bubble-gum in my hair, and the school's bully stole my clothes during physical education class. I was always the one sent to the office or suspended from school for standing up for myself. Fights occurred on the bus for no apparent reason. However, today, during my reminiscence regarding my school years, I realize that I might have been imagining that every time one of my classmates or a student from another grade level smiled at me that they really didn't know I had been molested, and by a preacher. The idea of a preacher breaking his promise to God to love and protect the people and children of God was difficult for me to accept.

I have always considered myself intellectually astute, but my grades declined because I was always sick or suspended from school. The inability to sleep at night was a factor as well. Luckily, there were only six weeks of school left. Mom conferenced with the principal and my teachers, who agreed to let me communicate with them in written format. But, so many nights, I lay awake wondering what piece of chocolate I had to eat the next day. I hated to see daylight. All I wanted to do was go someplace where no one knew my name; I could just end it all.

I couldn't outrun the nightmares and anxiety attacks. I was afraid to sleep because I knew hell would come alive in my dreams. Anxiety was my best friend. My therapist worked hard to get me up, out and about, but I couldn't. It took every ounce of energy I had to attend school. And I was angry with God too. I blamed Him for everything that happened to me! He ordained preachers and elders. I wanted the Traveling Elder dead, but God kept Him alive. He heard me crying through the night. He knew I had stopped eating and chose to be silent, a coping skill only I could control. Suicide was still in the back of my mind. It felt like that would be the only way I would get some peace.

The inability to sleep and frequent illness and stress caused my blood pressure to move into a medical danger zone; eighteen years old with a blood pressure of 170/90 to 208/100. I was in turmoil! My mind was so mixed up! I couldn't sleep, and I didn't want to eat. I was miserable. My doctor prescribed medication to control my blood pressure and anxiety. Unfortunately, the meds added to the problem. I stopped eating the right foods and binged on comfort foods. My inability to sleep became a significant problem, resulting in my falling asleep at school. I didn't want to go to school because it was uncomfortable; bullying and ugly remarks were on the daily agenda. So, I would use sickness as an excuse to be absent from school.

Although I was angry with God, my spiritual beliefs remain strong. I believed in Him, and I tried so hard to please him. However, I struggled with *John 3:16; "For God so loved the world, that he gave his only begotten Son…"* I was perishing in my state of mind, and God left me alone to fight my battles.

Eventually, I stopped eating solid foods. My diet includes apple juice, white grape juice, and root beer.

One Sunday afternoon our minister came to visit me because I had stopped attending church. I didn't trust or believe him at all. He was a mixed-up preacher like the demon. Furthermore, I quit attending church because I was too weak. I wasn't eating solid food; my body was slowly breaking down. Rev. Hall read *Psalms 130*, verse five; *"I wait patiently for the Lord; my soul expectantly waits."* Then he turned to me and said he knew the community gossip was hard to hear but hold on and don't give up. Unfortunately, he was too late; the gossipers had made a believer out of me.

But the passage of scripture, "I will wait patiently for the Lord ..." stuck with me. As stated earlier, I was angry with God because He didn't punish The Traveling Elder. He was still alive, and I wanted him dead. However, I was waiting and hoping God would rewrite my disastrous story any day. Then my pastor said, "I know just how you feel." I lost it! What did he mean, he knew how I felt? Had someone molested him? Did he have to fight to make it in school? Had he ever been classified as a "mute" during his life span? It pissed me off for him to try and relate to me, especially when he didn't know the whole story.

I must have passed out, because when I realized something had happened, mom was talking and telling me that I almost choked on my vomit. I was wet with perspiration, and my body shook uncontrollably when I came out of whatever had happened to me. Someone called 911, and they took me to the emergency room. The doctor on duty ordered an INJECTION and admitted me to the hospital. I slept through to the next day. My friend, mother, and mom were praying for me when I awakened.

My mother cleaned house for a doctor (Harris) who had

her own counseling business. She was a kind Caucasian woman, and she tried to do everything possible to make things better for mom, especially me. My mother told her about the many issues I was encountering and that my doctor had suggested that I see a counselor or psychiatrist. So, Dr. Harris encouraged me to talk with a therapist on her staff. I explained that I was already seeing a therapist at the University of Alabama (it was old *Hillman Hospital at that* time) in Birmingham. I told her that I had been diagnosed with situational anxiety and depression, and I eased in that I might have PTSD due to past trauma.

Before my therapist left for maternity leave, she suggested that I stay out of school for a while. Unfortunately, she entered early labor, and I was assigned a male therapist. I refused to see him. My original therapist called checking on me while she was on maternity leave several times, but it wasn't productive. But she did tell me something that stuck with me, "The only true threat you have, Ann is yourself. Give therapy a try again. If you find it too emotional, you don't have to return."

The doctor released me on Tuesday; Mom and I saw a therapist in Dr. Harris's office the following Monday. She told us right away that she was a Christian. I didn't care about that. Also, she suggested that I see her three times a week, once with Mom and twice alone. My first-time impression was that I didn't care for her. She asked me how it made me feel when the people I trusted hurt me, and she tried to tell me how I should work hard to overcome the letdown and try to forgive them. I didn't want to forgive the demon; I wanted him *dead*! I wasn't interested in her intellectual, looking down her nose at me jargon. So, I went to my sessions, sat there, and let her talk. During what I think was the fifth session, she asked if I ever thought about the man who violated me? That was too much. I ran to the car and told Mom I was not going back to therapy. Mom and I went back inside, sat together, and talked about her approach to my situation. She gave an in-depth explanation of why she asked me that particular question. I understood, and I continued my treatment with her.

On our way home from the ninth session, we saw The Traveling Elder! He walked across the streets to the cafe directly in front of my therapist's office. He stopped, standing in the doorway of the café looking across toward her office. He saw Mom and me when we got into our car. I crouched down in the seat, hoping he wouldn't see me, but he did. When he was arrested for continuing his despicable full body rub downs of other girls and was sentenced to seven years in prison, I couldn't ever bring myself to believe that the sentence matched his *crimes*. What was he doing out and over near my therapist's office? Had he been stalking us? Me? Mom panicked and called Dad, who insisted that we stay put and he would come to us immediately. While we were waiting in the car, The Traveling Elder came over to our car. He leaned into the window, with those dark, empty black holes for eyes, still trying to take control of my soul. Before he could say a word, the police officers apprehended him and took him away.

Just the thought of him on the streets made me physically ill. The headaches came back, and the anxiety attacks were worse than ever. I tried to sleep in my room, but it was impossible. I didn't sleep at all that night. To be honest, I crawled in the bed with mom and dad. He got up and let me sleep with mother and moved to the guest room.

I was doing so well in therapy too. Why did he come back? I couldn't clear the threat that monster imposed on me out of my head; telling me what he could do and how easy it would be for him to execute. How did he know how to find mom and me at the therapist office? Is he stalking me? Why did he stand in the doorway of the café? Was he trying to prove to me that he could find me, it didn't matter where or what time of day or night? Was he sending a message that there was no place I could go to hide from him? I wasn't trying to hide. We all thought he was still in prison. His actions were bold and smug. And for those reasons, I *am positive he would follow through* and do what he said he would do if given the opportunity. So, my parents prepared an area in their room for me to sleep in every night. I felt safer if dad were in the room with momma and me, especially at night.

Eventually, I started attending school. I still couldn't focus; sitting for an exam and getting a passing score was unlikely. I was always one step from having an anxiety attack. Tired and sleepy all the time.

I was braving the storm until The Traveling Elder showed up. I had a four-day school week. I even went to a few football games. We were all pleased at my progress. But after seeing the demon, my company keepers were feelings of embarrassment, emptiness, invisibility, hurt, betrayal, loneliness, and, most importantly, *FEAR!* Yes, I was eighteen, but I was *afraid for my life in so many ways!* **Fear is real. Not only is it real, but it has energy and lives inside your mind and heart!** To everyone reading this short story, it doesn't matter if friends and family surround you; you still *feel emptiness, feelings of invisibility, betrayal, loneliness,* and, the most emotional one for me was *fear.* **These are real live feelings.** The drama I experienced in school and the neighborhood gossip stole my life. I was afraid all the time. My energy, self-worth, and the desire to fight for my life were gone. *Fear took over!*

Before The Traveling Elder reappeared, mom and I had discussed with the therapist the possibility of cutting down on my schedule visits. But the shock of seeing that tall, long silky salt and peppered hair demon with dark holes for eyes, brought everything back to life again. It felt like it had just happened the day we saw him on the streets.

All the time my therapist and I spent together; we haphazardly built a respectful, solid relationship. I trusted and respected her suggestions. It wasn't easy for me to trust again, even females. So, when she suggested that I cut back on my scheduled time with her, I didn't agree. I wasn't sure why she thought I needed to cut back. Selfishly, she had worked with me whenever I needed her, including my regularly scheduled visits. She knew how hard and long I had been working trying to improve my physical and emotional health, and the progress I had made. She may have thought it was time to wean me off the intravenous lifeline attached to the weekly therapy sessions in her office. She told me she thought I could do it on my own. But I didn't agree! She had parked her car on the wrong dam side of the road with that one …

Although everyone that knew I was seeing a therapist commented that it seemed like I was doing well and ready to move on with my life, but that was the farthest from the truth of the matter. Life at that time wouldn't allow me to stop seeing my therapist. Some days I completed homework assignments with her because I continued to *have problems sleeping at night because the fear of the demon coming to get me had been rekindled; I believed he would take me away.*

Also, I couldn't focus at night trying to study which impacted any daytime studies, especially at school. Finally, during the tenth session, I *spoke aloud.* During the previous session, I communicated with my therapists in writing. Sometimes we played with some of her special figures, but most communication was with pen and paper. I shared what hurt me the most; people say I am defective and damaged goods. I realize that everybody is flawed somehow, and we don't know their flaws. But because The Traveling Elder was arrested and jailed, I believed everybody knew what happened, and that took my dignity away.

She took my hand and said, "you are right, Anne; we are all flawed. But if you decide to believe street gossip, why not consider this? I am beautifully imperfect, and it doesn't matter what the flaw is; I am still beautiful inside and out because God made me in His image". Wow! What a lightning bolt! I felt different, a presence was in the room, but I was afraid to tell her because I thought she would think I was a real nut case about to jump off the ledge.

During the eleventh session, my therapist asked me what I wanted to be in life. I was snappy and answered that just because I was adopted and molested doesn't mean I will be "a nobody!" She just smiled. I apologized and said I see myself nurturing adopted children, victims, and survivors of sexual abuse and molestation. Why do you want to help these people? Is it because you …, she stopped talking and smiled. I stopped talking, too. Finally, she asked if I knew that the House of Hope housed homeless mothers, children, and women who had been sexually abused or molested. Sometimes they provide shelter for trafficked girls. That got my attention, and we ended the session by discussing my possibilities as a part-time employee at the center.

I was in the Chapel praying when the center's director, Mrs. Spain walked in. She verified who I was and then offered me a job at The House of Hope on Wednesday and Friday after school. How did she know I was interested in a job at the center? Had my therapist told her about our conversation? If so, what else did she tell her about me? Then, I thought about what if the monster finds out that I am working after school at the House of Hope? What if he's roaming around outside somewhere and takes me.

I was so angry because I had to live in fear of this monster named The Traveling Elder. If he had just stayed away from me, I could have lived a normal life as a teenager; everything would have been so different. But my parents couldn't see him for the beast he was. They revered preachers, bishops, elders, and anyone who said they were a man of God!
      "After I talk with my parents, I will let you know if I take

the job," Mrs. Spain. "Take your time," she said. "I will save the opening for you whenever you are ready." Talking with Mom and Dad was refreshing. They agreed to be outside The House of Hope early every evening after work. I was so excited about this opportunity. It was my dream to work with at-risk families. I felt happy inside!

Finally, graduation! What a great feeling that was. My mentor teacher made graduation possible for me. I didn't have to face another day of insults and bullying. And I was proud of myself because I finished nine exams in 5 hours and 32 minutes. After testing was complete, we spent a few minutes talking. She told me that sometimes circumstances ignite unbearable pain on the inside; sometimes, you even have thoughts of suicide (the *molestation advocated the idea many times*).

Mrs. Spain, shared with me that she, too, was diagnosed with seasonal depression and bipolar disorder after her husband passed away. It was an interesting conversation lasting about thirty minutes. Then she said emphatically, *"Ann always knows that God is more potent than any medicine."* Our talk was motivating. I felt like I could make it through the dark, depressing days ahead if more were to come.

Finally, something good was happening in my life. Am I finally on the right track? Is God teaching me how to allow my past to help mold and shape me for my future? That night was the first whole night's sleep without nightmares that I could remember in four years. Although my religious foundation was Apostolic, as a teenager, all I wanted to do was finish high school and get the hell out of Montevallo.

However, I did understand that without God, I had no purpose, no destiny. Questions that clouded my mind often were, "does God allow brokenness? Does He allow bad things to happen to you to prove a point? Will He watch you fall to pieces so He can put you back together? Is this what my life going to be like to force me to become a solid witness of his goodness?" I didn't have the brain space to entertain that thought.

God Will Show Up and Show Out

Everything happens for a reason. So, the critical question one should ask themselves is, are you prepared for the "thing/s" that caused something to happen? I wasn't. It is 1967, the anxiety attacks and nightmares have slowly dissolved. I am married and expecting our first child, and I have one more quarter left in nursing school. Nursing school was never my career of choice. My passion has always been to work with sexually molested children, victims, and survivors of human trafficking. However, my mentor teacher paid for my schooling, so I became a nurse. I never accepted nursing as my career choice, although I would be helping others, but not in the areas I had envisioned. And, when it was time to sit for the nursing exam, I freaked out! I am not sure why I doubted my ability to do well on the exam because God had already proved himself to me when I passed nine exams in five hours with a score of ninety-five and above.

It wasn't a good time to start doubting my intellectual abilities; allowing fear to rule. It was a simple nursing exam! I've pondered this question many times; if the residue of fear flowing through my veins and doubting myself was because I really didn't want to pass the exam. Deep down inside, I realized that I was about to embark on a new journey with fear and anxiety as the pilot. Were these my true nemesis? Of all the emotional, physical, and health issues I encountered, the most upsetting of all my nemesis were the fear of The Traveling Elder being released or breaking out of prison.

I tried several times to find out if he were still imprisoned, but I couldn't locate any information about him. It was like he vanished from the face of the earth. And I was not comfortable asking for legal assistance for fear that my husband would find out. I didn't want him to know that I was still allowing my thoughts of this monster following through on his threat to continue hindering me from moving forward in a positive light. But the idea *never escaped the pleats in my brain.*

I continued on the path of nursing for twelve years. Finally, the anxiety and medical hindrances rolled over to my marriage. It was one illness right behind the other. Eight months after our first child was born, I suffered a ruptured appendix, an inflamed gallbladder that resulted in an emergency cholecystectomy and appendectomy. My husband was an educator in Shelby County, and he couldn't take off work every time I needed him. So, my mother moved in with us. That was a relief for my husband and me.

Anxiety attacks occurred sometimes three or four times a day. Because I was breastfeeding, I couldn't take *strong* anxiety medication. I was a miserable person. My obstetrician diagnosed me with post-partum depression. Thank God the medicine he prescribed for that illness helped with the anxiety, and it wasn't harmful to the baby.

Four months later, we found out that I was three months pregnant, and that same Friday evening, we celebrated our son's first birthday. That was a fantastic day. Our son Maya didn't understand what was happening, but he was jumping, goo-gooing and having fun in his one-year-old world. That same night my husband had to referee a basketball game. Additionally, it was my weekend to work from eleven at night to seven the following day. When I left for work that night, I noticed a car pulling out behind me. It wasn't a big deal because our street was active.

The drive from my house to St. Margaret's was about 2.5 miles. Although it was late evening, I wasn't afraid because I traveled this route without incident. So, the vehicle traveling behind me wasn't a concern. However, when I stopped for the red light, the driver stayed at a distance. My fuel light flashed, so I pulled into the gas station close to my house. My husband always fussed because I would allow the fuel to get low in my car before refueling. He reminded me that I didn't need to stop at night to gas the car. He was correct!

The driver of the mystery vehicle pulled in too. Something didn't feel right. Remember I said earlier that there are consequences for every choice you make? Stopping at the gas station that night was the wrong choice! But I didn't have another option. The gentlemen got out of his car, looking in my direction. I never turned my back to him, but when I attempted to place the pump back in the tank holder, he walked up behind me, put a gun to my head, and told me to be quiet, stay calm, and get in the car. Someone must have been watching and called the police.

He was shouting, "Now who's the boss? I can splatter your brains all over this cement, and I wouldn't spend one night in jail because I'm mentally ill. You would be just another dead "nigger". I had never seen this person before. I was screaming for the station attendant to help me, but he locked the door to the store. But I am quite sure he was the one that notified the police. Suddenly I started repeating, "I put my trust in God, and I am not afraid." That agitated Carl E. Finally, six police officers surrounded us, but Carl E. didn't remove the gun from my head. I was pleading with him to let me go. I am pregnant; please don't hurt me. At the same time, the police officers were yelling out commands too, and his anxiety escalated. Yelling out, "I'll shoot her, get back!" I started repeating the exact phrase, and Carl E. got angrier and more anxious.

The police officers yelled at me to stop talking, but I knew God was with me because my body felt lite, and I could feel myself calming down. Then Carl E. took the gun away from my head and let go of my shirt but told me to stand still. He stood there looking around; I thought he was going to surrender. But suddenly, he snatched me backward, placed the gun to my head, yelling, "Get back, I'll kill her!" He jerked me from his left side to his right side, back and forth, peering from behind me, watching the officer's reaction to his behavior. Three officers start walking our way from different vantage points. Then Carl E. took the gun from my head and pointed it at my stomach. Trying to stay aware of each officer's position, he became more agitated. He wanted to use me as a shield, so he yanked me with the gun on my stomach in front of him, but I lost my footing and fell backward on the pavement. That's when I heard a loud boom, then he fell to the ground next to my face, blood gushing from his head and mouth.

A female officer immediately helped me up and walked me to her car. I was cramping in the lower part of my stomach, so the ambulance transported me to the hospital. I stayed that night and the next day under obstetrical observation. I found out later that Carl E. had been a patient one night I worked in the emergency room at St. Margaret's Hospital. He wanted pain medication. But he was a frequent flyer, shopping hospitals pretending to be in pain to get drugs. So, I discharged him without giving him pain medication. The security guard informed me later that Carl E. had been seen outside the hospital a few nights before the incident.

My life and my baby's life were in danger. But God's presence exuded even amid evil and craziness. He covered us that horrible night. Proverbs 8:14 talks about the fear of the Lord are our strength. We were in the *Shadows of Death*, but God's love and grace delivered us; he still expected me to walk in the life He designed for me before I was born.

Dancing In the Rain with A Purpose

Three weeks after the incident, I was assigned to work on the medical- surgical unit. During my rounds that night, I entered a patient's room who had surgery that day to remove his gallbladder. He had post anesthesia snaps. When I entered the room, he was out of bed trying to remove the IV from his arm. When I approached him, he managed to kick me in the stomach which sent me backwards falling over a chair. I knew immediately that I was in trouble. I lost our little girl the following day!

After that unkind loss, I worried if I would be a good mother and make the right decision when it came to our children. I seem to have taken on the full responsibility as protector because Johnny worked out of town and wasn't home until Friday evening and right back on the road again Monday morning. Therefore, I was the protector for five days and nights. But I should have known to call for assistance when I walked in the patient's room and found him out of bed and agitated. But I didn't. I was concerned about him. That moment of concern for others caused me the life of my child.

The loss of our little girl made me overly protective of our one-year-old. I was determined that I would make the best decision and keep him safe by any means necessary. The holy-oil incident still haunted me. I didn't allow anyone to touch his cheeks or kiss him on his hands. I was obsessed with protecting him from evil people. I didn't have any reason to believe that my family would harm my baby, but I was cautious of them as well. On the contrary, my parents trusted the monster that changed my life. So, fragments of my molestation lingering in the fissures of my mind was the ethos behind my strong obsession to protect my children. It wore on my nerves all the time.

Our marriage was great, the baby was fine, and we lived a simple financial life, counting pennies occasionally. But for some reason, I just couldn't get it together! As time progressed, my husband's commute to Montevallo every Monday and back to Montgomery every Friday evening became a financial concern. Money was low, and gas wasn't free. So significant sacrifices had to be made to ensure that money was available.

We discussed the idea of both of us taking a second job. But with the baby needing twenty-four-hour attention and my husband being away all week and traveling back home on the weekends, and I was already working swing shift; three to eleven and sometimes eleven to seven, we felt it wouldn't be healthy or feasible for either of us or the baby to work a second job. I didn't know how to really seek the Lord for specific needs, I just prayed hoping He would give me an answer. Six months after the discussion about taking on a second job, I was offered a permanent shift position at St. Margaret's Hospital. The adjustment wouldn't be difficult because I was already working swing shift sometime. And I would make more money working eleven to seven also.

I worked the night shift and slept most of the day. Although my mother lived with us, it still didn't leave much personal time for myself or my husband or the baby. I felt guilty; I robbed him of intimate time with me, but he never complained. I know God had to design him for me. Any other husband would have left me pregnant and alone with a one-year-old. But my husband was and remains my solid rock! He knew I was depressed and that I was miserable at work. He was aware that the anxiety attacks were back again. No nightmares, just anxiety uproars. But he was my biggest cheerleader!

As stated early on, I never wanted to be a nurse. I felt in my heart that my purpose in life was working with at-risk individuals. However, if nursing was my ministry, I never received affirmation from God through prayer or a dream.

While the anxiety fits continued to wreak havoc on my mental state, I had surgery to remove my right kidney and six cancerous tumors. My temperature stayed elevated which resulted in an extended stay in the hospital. *How much longer will I be tormented? I can't take much more Lord! I am tired!* I just wanted peace in a few areas of my life. But is seem as though I was hindering my own peace. I just couldn't get it together! I started to believe that because I was sick most of the time, that God had to be punishing me for something.

My best friend knew I wasn't at peace, but we never talked about it. She would come over and help my mother with housekeeping and the baby, but we never talked about my emotions and how I really felt. She was a great friend, a dependable person. The day I was discharged from the hospital she was there to help me get settled. But I couldn't bring myself to talk about my true feelings with her. She didn't know about the molestation; well, I didn't think so!

When it was time for me to be discharged, I made all kinds of excuses to keep her from coming over. I wasn't ready for her mouth. Sometimes she didn't know when to stop beating a dead horse. But she came on as planned. At first, it angered me, then I fell in her arms and cried. I felt so lost and alone. I couldn't tell my husband how I felt. He would be disappointed because I had already told him things were good. I expected my friend to understand and help me recover from the mental fog in my head. Rightly so, because she had a doctorate in counseling, she was a Certified Life Coach, and a "real" minister. Instead, she said, *"You look like a mess! Didn't you have your makeup kit with you at the hospital? What happened to you?"* That hurt me deeply and broke my spirit, and I burst into tears.

Eventually she said, *"Anne, what we want is not always what God wants for us. He will hold back what we desire so He can prepare us for what we need."* She knew I didn't want to be a nurse and why I chose it as a career. I listened as she ministered to me. As the morning progressed, she apologized for her abrasive tone and the comment regarding my appearance (*I did look a mess*). Before she left, my house was in order, she prepared a big meal because my husband was coming in for the weekend, and she made sure my mother knew where she placed the clothes she washed. My friend was a blessing to me that miserable day. She brought light where there was darkness.

So did God send her my way to help me understand that His plans would come to fruition in due season, and they would prosper?

Fifteen months after the fourth surgery, I started feeling sick again. The anxiety attacks were slowly creeping back. I finally saw a doctor; he diagnosed me with tonsillitis, and I had a tonsillectomy. I spent numerous hours in and out of the emergency room, sometimes admitted, sometimes treated, and sent home.

Frequent visits to the emergency room is usually a red flag for nurses; is this person shopping for drugs? However, working a permanent night shift and occasional swing shifts, the emergency nurses didn't know I was a night supervisor, *and I was ashamed to make it known.* I tried to handle my illness alone by not disclosing my feelings to my husband. But keeping them a secret almost became fatal. Anxiety and depression were in control; I thought about ending my life many times. God had to be punishing me because of some choice I made. I wanted it all to stop! Stress HURTS!

We relocated to Montevallo because of my health. Our home was located one mile from my husband's worksite. And, since I was having recurrent health issues, it was a financially safe move. In September 1972, we were pregnant again. I knew the medication would be harmful to the baby, so I made a medical decision I wasn't qualified to make; I took myself off of the medicine. Without medication, I lived six horrible months of anxiety hell. Then Satan started playing games with my mind! Imaginative experience, I heard a whisper in my right ear. God was trying to prepare me for what was coming, but I didn't understand it at that time.

A year post-delivery, the excitement about returning to work was gone, and I wanted to move out of our small town. So,

I started a job search in Birmingham. I continue chasing after the purpose someone else chose for me. Thus, in October 1974, we relocated to Fairfield, and I accepted a position at Community Hospital. I didn't consult God about my decision. But my husband understood why relocating might be good for me, so he agreed with the move. Unfortunately, three months on the new job, blood clots started forming in my leg, breaking loose going to my lungs. Every three to four months, I was in the hospital with a clot in my lung. Talking about *losing my faith*, I even started to doubt if there was a supernatural being.

One night when I was journaling, I opened it to the following quote, "Gratitude is a powerful process for shifting your energy to more of what you want into your life. Be grateful for what you already have, and you will attract more good things." (Rhonda Byrne). I got aggravated and snapped at the writing on the page, *"I am grateful,"* I yelled out. Ashamed, I started to cry and beg God for forgiveness. *"I am trying Lord, I am trying! But I don't know what to do!"*

My husband heard my cries and came into the bedroom to check on me. *"What's happening?"* he asked. *"Are you alright?"* I thought about my friend and what she said about God's plan for our life. I fell in his arms crying and telling him what Barb said to me, "What we want is not always in God's plans. Sometimes our plans get tangled up, so God can prepare us for what we need." *"Do you think this is what going on with me?"* I asked. My wonderful husband just held me in his strong arms which made me feel safe. I don't know what that was all about. I wasn't thinking of the demon that night. It had been twenty plus years; he should be dead paying for his evil deeds in hell by now.

What a revelation! Here I am complaining and agonizing over being a nurse. Instead, I should be thankful I have a job! Sadden over my complaining, I fell to my knees and began praying. I heard a soft voice saying, "Let me help you." It had to be God; my family didn't know I was awake, not even my husband! God wanted me to understand that He was aware of my issues. He knew I was suffering! And He knew Satan wanted me to doubt Him and make me take my life. But I didn't understand why He wouldn't come to my rescue! I spent the remainder of the night curled up in my chair, dismal and agitated.

One health condition forced me to seek the help of several doctors. I lost weight, my body ached, *I was just SICK*! I had numerous x-rays, gastrointestinal exams, and radiation exposure, is what I remember. The doctors didn't do a pregnancy test because I had a tubal ligation after our second child was born. So, I couldn't be pregnant.

My therapist increased my medication every time I saw her. When women frequently complain of not feeling well, some doctors automatically think we are weird or crazy. Finally, I went back to my obstetrician, the one who refused to do the tubal ligation in the first place. After a pregnancy test and an examination, he informed me that I was three months pregnant. March 15, 1976, I delivered our third bundle of joy, TKM, our little princess.

Twelve weeks of maternity leave allowed my legs to rest. I was confident the clots would dissolve. Sadly, they continued to invade my lungs and I had to extend my maternity leave out four more months. There were times I started to believe it was God's will for me to suffer. My health continued to decline. I couldn't work or take care of my children. My mother was in-house; she took over the primary operations to keep everything afloat. Eventually, my strength returned, and I went back to nursing. My legs started swelling and getting sore again. I would sometimes experience severe shortness of breath. Off to the emergency room praying that another clot had not broken loose and found its way to my lungs.

Finally, my doctor recommended finding a job that would

allow me to control my mobility. Unfortunately, there were no such jobs. Another relocation, back to Montevallo. Again, a safe financial move. With my doctor's input, I qualified for disability. Disability opened the door to Vocational Rehabilitation Service (VRS). Through VRS, I had the financial resources to pursue a degree in any area I desired. I chose education. I prayed about it before deciding to move forward, but I didn't wait to hear from God.

Sporadic health issues while attending school were complex. Withal, in 1982 I graduated from college with a BS in Elementary Education and an endorsement in Criminal Justice. I wasn't sure why I chose Criminal Justice as an endorsement. But it was useful later in life. I taught school during the day and worked towards a master's in counseling at night. Some of my acquaintances and friends believed I was wasting time pursuing a degree in counseling because there were no counselors in elementary schools during that time. But in 1989, I earned a master's in counseling. And because I was diagnosed with situational depression and anxiety, I earned certification in Behavioral Techniques in 1990. Will counseling be my niche? Is this why I am here on earth? If so, I took a twelve-year detour.

My health was a constant nightmare. I was still taking medication for depression three times a day and anxiety meds at night. Medication coupled with a nervous stomach and almost no sleep made it challenging to concentrate. Nevertheless, I continued teaching, and my health continued to decline. My first-year teaching, I had a mass removed from my breast and three surgeries on my left foot. The only time I left Montevallo was to see a doctor. *Where is God? Nothing is working for me. Everything I touch falls apart!*

My prayer, partner who was my best friend, and I met for lunch. She knew everything about my situation. I talked about my depression and how disappointed I was because I didn't realize I was wasting time getting a degree in counseling.

"I should have chosen another area of focus. I don't want to teach school for the rest of my life," I said. "I want to work closely with the at-risk population."

She stopped me and asked when had I spent intimate time with God *dissecting the real issue*? She didn't let me answer. Instead, for an hour or so, we prayed together and talked about how to get intimate with God.

"Have you given God everything from your past and let go of the hatred you still carried in your heart, Ann?" I got angry and left without saying goodbye. We met in the choir room that Sunday, and I apologized for my attitude.

During church, I developed an excruciating headache. The following Wednesday, I was admitted to the hospital with a stroke. I told my husband, *"This is it! I know God wants me dead or crazy!"* I shouldn't have made that statement because He showed me what hell could be like on earth. While pursuing my doctorate, I had a stroke, two aneurysms removed from the right side of my brain, and a thyroidectomy seven months after the aneurysm surgery.

Three hours of sleep was the nightly routine. I would awaken during the night drenched with sweat and my heart would be racing. Before my mother passed away, I'd go into her room and lie on the floor beside her bed, trying to go back to sleep. I continued to think that I would be better off if I were dead! My family could get on with their life. But God wasn't going to let me get by that easy.

In 1991 Alabama Board of Education added counselors to elementary schools. I was thrilled that I had pursued a master's in counseling. I applied for the position where I was teaching, but I didn't get the job. But another job came available, and I got that position. I was in my classroom, packing up to relocate, is when

I finally understood God's voice. "I've been by your side all the time. I saw you, but you didn't recognize me." I knew it was Him because I'd heard that voice many times before, but I didn't have the insight to know it was Him. Proverbs 16:3 came to mind, a scripture my mother often talked about, "Commit your works to the Lord, and your plans will be established." But I gave God control the night of the near-death incident. We connected! His presence was all around me!

I tried to continue packing, but I was disturbed! Not anxious, but my spirit wasn't comfortable. Tears were flowing, and I didn't know why. I could hear my friend when she asked if I had told God everything? I don't ever remember coming clean about my struggles over the years and blaming Him for keeping the pedophile alive. I collapsed! I didn't faint; my legs just wouldn't hold me up! But that's where God wanted me, on the floor! I had to submit myself to Him exclusively.

Stretched out on my classroom floor, I begged God to teach me how to forgive. I petitioned Him for forgiveness for disrespecting Him and blaming him for my messed-up life. I needed His purpose for my life to go forth. The only way that would happen was for me to forgive those that hurt me! When I got home, my husband and children were at a football game. I fell to my knees. I needed God to heal me where I hurt the most, on the inside! So, I sought Him on a different level. Finally, after several hours of crying and praying, I knew my heart was right with God, and my spirit, soul, and body aligned with Him. He healed me on the inside that Friday night! Hallelujah!

My husband orchestrated the move to my office at Thompson. So, finally, here I am, God, executing the purpose you designed for me. The calm atmosphere was unbelievable. The time I spent at The House of Hope was the beginning of this special moment, the work God destined for me to accomplish. It helped mold me for the office in which I was standing. And time with the at-risk population was instrumental in helping me accept the unfavorable events in my life and know that there was hope.

On my purpose-designed journey, I earned an associate degree in nursing, a master's and an Educational Specialist Degree in Counseling and Behavioral Psychology, a Doctorate Degree in Educational Administration, Certification in Behavioral Techniques, Certified Date Rape Counselor, and a graduate from the Police Academy. Also, I am the face of Survivors Rock, Inc., a Virtual Community assisting survivors and victims of sexual molestation, human trafficking, date rape and spousal abuse (**https://www.theycandance.com**).

Currently, I am authoring a book about a little girl born into a family of sexual molesters and human traffickers. And I have counseled homeless mothers, teenagers, and women who felt useless because of their past and current lifestyle. Also, I've placed women and children in Safe Places trying to escape abusive situations. I have rescued several young ladies whose boyfriend dumped them beside the interstate or a country road because they would not succumb to his sexual demands. That's my purpose in life; helping people.

To change the trajectory of my life, I had to release the distractors; (*hate, unforgiveness, a loss of self-worth, doubt, and fear*) that were hindering me from efficaciously living the life God purposed explicitly for me. I learn to value my worth.

I understand now that some diamonds are imperfect, but they never lose their value. Whatever happens, I will always be a diamond in God's eyesight. Also, I had to FORGIVE the people that hurt me. It wasn't easy because forgiving is a choice, not a feeling. However, spending intimate time with God taught me how to forgive!

I learned to Dance in the Rain with a Purpose by trusting God and knowing that He is always where I need Him to be. It is comforting to know that you are never alone, and that God always works for your good in His own time and on His terms. "This is what purpose-driven living is all about. ~ Rick Warren Points to remember; (1). The more you can forgive and let go of the past, the more room you have to receive God's favor in your life. (2) Absolute submission to God is necessary if you wish to live a purpose-filled life. (3). Get to know God's voice. It is crucial, especially when you are in a precarious situation. (4). Know your passion. It will help you figure out God's purpose for your life.

I am sharing my intimate story to highlight the goodness of God in the life He purposed for me. Also, I hope readers are inspired to learn how to love themselves no matter what comes their way. Learn how to live despite your flaws, mistakes, and failures. Seek God's guidance in finding out who you are in Him. That's how I Learned How to Dance in the Rain with a Purpose! It changed the trajectory of my life.

Meet Dr. Annie R. McClain

Dr. Annie R. McClain is the founder and Chief Executive Officer of Survivors Rock, Inc., a faith based nonprofit virtual community that serves victims and survivors of commercial sex trafficking, rape, and extreme relationship abuse. She is the empathetic, proactive, poised, multi-talented, strong professional voice for the abused and maltreated. Annie serves on the Board of Directors as well. As CEO of Survivors Rock, Inc., she leads a Team of professionals in developing and delivering transformational and innovative techniques to encourage victims and survivors to take back the control of their physical, mental, and emotional environment and learn to live a purpose driven life, regardless of their dysfunctional past. Because of various personal experiences, Annie found inspiration for the formation of the nonprofit. A short-term goal is to establish a land-based facility.

Before the founding of Survivors Rock, Inc., as a first-grade instructor, hands-on experience with privileged and underprivileged children was a conduit to expanding her professional background. She served elementary and middle school students and their families as school counselor for thirteen years, while volunteering as a rape an at-risk counselor in the Birmingham area. Also, Annie worked as a volunteer counselor at a Safe House for women seeking time away from physical, sexual, and or financial abuse. Annie rescued several teen girls when they were abandoned alone on the roadside by their significant others when they would not succumb to their sexual demands.

As principal of Montevallo Elementary School, she was responsible for leading her staff in planning and implementing strategic educational opportunities for the students and transforming the lives of underprivileged and abused students as well. Annie's career choices and accomplishments were many but educational and exciting. They include the formation of Survivors Rock, Inc, former registered nurse, police officer, at-risk counselor, teacher, principal, and an author. She earned a master's degree in education with an endorsement in criminal justice, master's degree and an educational specialist degree in counseling, associate degree in nursing, and a doctorate in educational administration.

Dr. McClain enjoys having fun with her family, reading, traveling, shopping, and helping others. She is a believer in the power of prayer and renewing of the mind. Walking with God, professional and individual experiences, advanced academics, and post-graduate studies in psychology and behavioral counseling afford her the knowledge, expertise, purpose, and skills to Dance in the Rain with a Purpose.

Bruised Not Broken
Tracy M. Dorsey

I can't believe I'm sitting here.

I was actually in the waiting room of a therapist's office, expecting my name to be called. That was the kind of thing I saw other people, mainly white people, doing on television. As I sat there imagining the faces of people who had sat in this chair before, I found myself thinking about the tragic life events or even addictions that led each of them here.

Kleptomaniac. Agoraphobic. Eating Disorder. Marital issues.

They probably were not necessarily crazy or criminal. I wasn't. Well, not certifiably, anyway. I guessed a lot of them came here for the same reason I did. Just to talk and hopefully get some help. I certainly needed help dealing with all the anger, resentment, hurt, and huge hole of emotional debt that had made me spiritually bankrupt. Sometimes, I felt like a hamster spinning on a wheel in its cage, going round and round but never getting anywhere no matter how hard its tiny feet tried.

I'm not the only person in the world who needs therapy. I'm just inexperienced.

When one of my best friends, Phaedra, first suggested that I *see* someone, I had a hunch she knew I would not be thrilled about the idea. After all, in my circle of girlfriends, I was always the strong one. I was the one everybody else came to for advice when they had a problem. I had all of my shit figured out, or at least I'd done a damn good job making it appear that way. The truth was I had everything in my life together except this.

"Okay girl, hear me out. I need you to be open to what I'm about to suggest. I think that maybe you should talk to someone," Phaedra said, nervously.
"Someone like who?"

"A therapist."

You think I'm nuts?

"What?" I screamed, almost strangling on my drink, "I don't need to talk to a two-hundred -and fifty dollar an hour head shrinker for help. All I need to do is just go to church and get my Jesus on. After that, I'll be all right," I finished, rolling my eyes, and dismissing her silly suggestion with the wave of my hand.

Maybe I should make an appointment with Pastor Hawkins. Couldn't hurt.

I pulled out my phone to make myself a note.

"Hey, I'm not knocking against going to church and praying," Phaedra began, "Lord knows I've prayed until it seemed I'd run out of words. But I also believe that God gave us doctors, and while I was on my knees praying, I asked him to send the right one to help me. Hannah, our people are dying inside and refusing to get help. We're just walking around suffering. Suffering ain't cute! The stigma we have about seeing a doctor for our mental health and wellness is partially responsible for what's keeping us crazy. The lives we lead are stressful. We are overworked, underpaid, overlooked, profiled, under-served, used, abused, denied, killed in the street, and our own damn bed...girl...do I need to go on?"

Deep down, I knew Phaedra was right. I could use a little couch time. If my goal was to become a whole, healthy woman, there was no way to avoid seeking professional help, and the longer I resisted, the pain would inevitably become unbearable. As I listened to Phaedra explain how therapy helped her to cope with the issues she had with her mother, I began to realize that we all have scars. Some scars are on the surface, barely breaking the skin. Others can be deep malignant wounds that choke the heart and suffocate the soul until neither is recognizable. I felt that.

When she was seven years old, Phaedra's crack-addicted mother sold her to a drug dealer for twenty dollars. After a couple of months of being forced to use drugs and being raped by his friends, the drug dealer abandoned Phaedra's battered body on the doorstep of a neighborhood church. She bounced from one foster home to another for three years before being adopted by a wonderful family. Phaedra never saw her mother again until the day she graduated from college. Out of the blue, her mom showed up, claiming sobriety, and looking for redemption.

The difference between Phaedra and I is that she eventually escaped from her childhood hell. I continued to burn in mine.

So, I finally took my friend's loving advice and there I was. Papers all filled out, waiting for my name to be called.

"Hannah Gilliard," I heard a voice call. I looked up, and saw a tall, thin, regal-looking woman standing in the doorway. Her smile was sympathetic as she looked in my direction.

Look at her. She is already judging my level of dysfunction.

I was escorted into a large round office that looked as if it had been designed specifically for the cover of *Architectural Digest* with a breathtaking view of the city. The textured walls held a collection of impressive art along with framed degrees from Columbia, Wellesley, and Howard. Everything, from the rich African mudcloth throws to the huge meticulously carved mahogany desk, appeared to have been collected from travels to an exotic destination.

Probably really Pier One.

"Hello, I'm Dr. Bryce. You can call me Jessica."

I smiled and nervously shook her extended hand. As I surveyed the room, I noticed something very important was missing. There wasn't a couch or even a chaise in sight. *This can't be a real therapist's office without a couch. Where am I supposed to fall out, kicking and screaming about all the heinous bullshit that had happened to me in my life?*

"Please sit down," the doctor said as she motioned toward two oversized cognac leather chairs in front of her desk.

"So, how are you?" Jessica asked.

"Okay," I answered, trying to look at ease.

She paused a moment and stared before continuing. *Awkward!*

"If you were okay, you wouldn't be here, would you?"

What the hell am I supposed to say?

"No, I guess not," I answered, trying hard not to sound sarcastic.

"Well, talk to me. What brings you here to see me?"

Jessica looked at me as if she could see clearly through to my shivering soul. Her eyes were as dark as midnight and as piercing as glass. She spoke barely above a whisper, probably on purpose so as not to startle the crazy into a violent outburst. Her gentle smile gave away the fact that she could sense my discomfort, despite my efforts to hide it. My body shifted in the buttery soft chair.

"I have a few issues I need help dealing with," I replied.

"Such as?"

"My mother," I said.

"Your mother? That's just one issue. You said that you have a few."

Seriously?

"My mother and her insipid attitude about me coming out about being molested by my stepfather," I answered, totally annoyed by this little game.

"I see," Jessica said, removing the turquoise-framed glasses from her golden oval-shaped face. She sat and watched me intensely for a moment as if waiting for me to burst into a never-ending puddle of tears. Been there, done that. In my thirty years, I had cried enough tears to quench the thirst of the population of several third-world countries and still would have enough water left over to end the drought in Georgia.

"First, I'd like to know more about you. What is Hannah's life like? Give me an example of a typical Hannah day. Tell me everything you did yesterday."

Say what now? I just told you I was molested by my stepfather, and you want to know what I did yesterday. I knew this was going to be a waste.

I didn't understand what any of this had to do with why I was here. Dr. Bryce only had an hour to fix me, and I was out of there.

But since I was paying for that hour, I reluctantly decided to humor her.

To describe my life as busy would be a gross

understatement. I am on the move from the moment my feet hit the floor at five in the morning until my head touches the pillow, usually sometime around midnight. My salon and spa require my constant attention. There are always situations to negotiate, dictate, or referee. But I adore what I do, and the satisfaction of knowing that I own and maintain my own successful business is well worth the aggravation.

I've always wanted to be Hannah Gilliard, Proprietress. The Gilly Salon and Spa has been vividly alive in me since I was twelve when I would paint the neighborhood girls' nails for fifty cents. After high school, I worked hard as a Spelman College student by day and a cosmetology school student at night. I did weaves and braids on the weekends to help pay for it. Once I had my business degree in one hand and my cosmetology license in the other, I was well on my way.

When The Gilly first opened its doors in the west end of the city, I was the only stylist. I juggled clients and bills like a one-arm circus performer. After six months, I was able to hire my teenage niece, McKenzie, to be my shampoo/receptionist/do girl for one hundred dollars a week. Little by little and prayer by prayer, the business grew tremendously. I now own a three-story building on the busiest street downtown and have twenty-seven full-time employees with benefits. The Gilly boasts a long list of celebrity clientele with a few notable politicians in the mix.

Sadly, the sweet smell of my success was often stifled by the painful memories of my childhood. My social life also suffered tremendously. My suspicious nature made it impossible to maintain intimate relationships with men. I would not allow myself to trust anyone because, in some way, they would eventually hurt or betray me. These experiences never changed. The longest relationship I'd ever had only lasted about three years. He was a good man. All he wanted to do was to love and take care of me. I just couldn't or wouldn't allow him to, probably because I didn't believe that I deserved it or I was just plain scared. I know that now.

As I gave her the details of my day, I couldn't tell if Jessica was interested in what I was saying because when she wasn't nodding aimlessly, she doodled away with her *Monte Blanc* on a yellow legal pad.

Old school.

When I was done talking, she handed me an appointment card to come back and chitchat again in a week.

"What's this?"

"An invitation to come back for another session."

Umm…no ma'am.

"How many more of these sessions do I need?"

"I don't know, Hannah. All of that really depends on you."

Stop talking to me in riddles and just tell me how to fix this.

"What does that mean?"

"It means that you are in control here. What you say and how often you need to say it until we begin dealing with the real is totally up to you."

"I thought you were just going to tell me what's wrong with me and what I need to do to fix it. You know, you'd write me a prescription, and I'd write you a check."

Jessica smiled and moved closer to me.
"Hannah, you are not paying me to fix you because you are not

broken," she began, "Objects get broken. People get bruised. A prescription will be just another crutch that will continue to allow you to limp away from the truth. I'm here to listen and ask the hard questions you have been too afraid to ask yourself. My methods can be a little, well… different but I do promise real results if you are willing to do the work."

Ugh! I hate this.

"So, see you next Tuesday," Jessica said as she walked toward the door, signaling my time was up.

I couldn't believe that I was actually using my hard-earned money and expensive insurance to pay someone to play with my head, but she was right. I really needed guidance to face this mountain, even if it meant weekly appointments with a shrinker.

During the next week's session, Jessica asked me to describe, in detail, the sexual abuse I suffered from my stepfather. I hadn't talked about it, I mean really talked about it, in a very long time. Speaking aloud about it was akin to reliving the horrible experiences again.

"Where was your birth father," she asked.

"He was killed in a car accident the night I was born. He was drunk and crashed into a sixteen-year-old girl head-on, killing her as well. All I know about him I learned from pictures and through the stories of others."

My mother met my stepfather two years later while visiting her cousin's church. They were married six months later. He was the only father I'd ever known. He was my daddy.

"The sudden marriage had to do with something about my mother not wanting to be alone, raising two children," I explained, "or so I've heard."

"Hannah, how old were you when the abuse began?"

"I was five years old."

"Do you remember the first time he raped you? Will you tell me about it?"

I took a deep breath and prayed for God to give me the strength I would so desperately need to go back to that painful place in order to get to the healing. It would take a miracle for me to get through this without crying like a baby. I closed my eyes and allowed my mind to stumble back to a time when my spirit became paralyzed, and my innocence was stolen.

It was a Saturday night. My mother had taken my older sister, Sarah, to the store. Sarah had been sick and acting weird all day. At the time, I didn't understand why or what was wrong with her. My mother just kept telling me to mind my own business.

"Sarah is growing up," she said, "One day you will understand."

I later realized Sarah had begun her period that day.

While my mother and sister were gone, I decided to pass the time by having a tea party with my dolls and stuffed animals. Shortly after they left, my stepfather came into my bedroom.

"Whatcha doing ladybug?" he asked, as he stood over me, smiling and playfully pulling one of my braided pigtails.

Since it wasn't an unusual thing for my stepfather to have a tea party with me, there was no need for me to feel fearful or suspect anything harmful would happen. I certainly couldn't have imagined anything like this.

We sat at my child-sized table, ate imaginary chocolate chip cookies, and pretended to drink tea from my toy china. Daddy even stopped what he was doing to go and put on a real necktie for the occasion, taking care to match my bubblegum pink boa and sparkly princess crown. We were having so much fun laughing at his big-person-on-tiny-furniture clumsiness and talking to my dolls as if they were real dinner guests. My daddy made a point to comment on how beautiful I was and what a big girl I was becoming. His undivided attention and unlimited compliments made me feel like a real princess.

"You know what, ladybug? I think that you are getting big enough to pretend to be Mommy. Wouldn't that be fun?" he asked as he held my small, gloved hand. "We can have a grown-up party. Just you and me."

Of course, it was the ultimate compliment for a little girl who idolized everything about her beautifully sophisticated mother. I was totally clueless as to what he really meant.

"Let's replace our pretend tea with mommy's favorite wine," he said as he left the room and returned to pour the deep red liquid into my cup.

The first sip made my tongue tingle and my throat burn.

"This is nasty, Daddy. I don't like it."

"Take another big sip," he encouraged to calm my visible distaste, "it will start to taste better."

My discomfort increased as the once innocent kiss on the forehead from my daddy became a sick seductive embrace from a grown man no little girl should ever experience. I was frightened by a dark urgency in his eyes that I'd never seen before as he held me tighter and pulled me closer.

"Daddy, what are you doing? You're hurting me," I cried. I felt dizzy and warm. It seemed to take longer for words to travel from my brain as they fumbled out of my mouth.

"Don't be scared, ladybug. This is just what it means to pretend to be Mommy. You have to do all of the things that mommy does to make daddy feel good. It will be much easier if you relax."

His heavy breathing was terrifying.

I tightly closed my eyes and cried out as I lay burning on my *Barbie* sheets. The stench of betrayal nauseated me, and I began to vomit uncontrollably with sadness and confusion. He continually growled at my mother's name with each excruciating thrust into my thin-framed body. My innocence evaporated and stained the pastel-colored walls of my room. That was the day my daddy became the big bad wolf stalking me in my own home. I was never the same.

Afterward, he gave me a warm bubble bath and told me I was now his special girl. He made me promise not to tell anyone about our new game of pretend, especially not my mother, because she may think I'm making fun of her, get angry, and spank me.

"How long did the abuse continue?" Jessica asked, jarring me.

In my seemingly long, vivid recollection of the past, I had almost forgotten someone else in the room.

"Until I got my period. I was twelve."

"Did you tell anyone about it?"

"No. Not until about a year ago."

"What happened a year ago?"

"The son of a bitch had a stroke and died."

When I reluctantly went home to help my mother and sister with the arrangements for the funeral, it was like returning to the scene of an unspeakable crime. Every room in the house held memories of being sexually violated in some way by the one man in the world I thought I was supposed to trust to protect me. So many people from the community spoke with only the highest respect and doting admiration for my stepfather. I became so upset and angry, I couldn't take another minute of being tortured again in that house. Later that evening, I told my mother about the hell my stepfather put me through, and she just stared blankly at me for a moment before insisting I was lying.

"I will not have you disrespect my dead husband's memory with your incredible lies, Hannah Marie Gilliard. You should be ashamed to come to me and even imply such blatant untruths."

"Mama, why would I lie about something like this?"

"I don't know. But let me make myself perfectly clear," she viciously threatened, "If you plan to continue to tell these tales about the man who has loved and cared for you since you were in diapers, you will never be allowed to step foot into this house, *his* house again. I won't have it!"

The cold hardness in my mother's grieving eyes broke my heart. It certainly was not the reaction I expected. Yeah, I'd imagined there would be a great deal of emotion about my truth, but the possibility of disbelief or banishment never entered my mind. My mama was supposed to always believe me. She, too, was supposed to love me. Fail.

While I was hastily packing my suitcase, my sister came to me and begged me not to leave. She said that she believed me because Daddy had done the exact same thing to her.

"Why didn't you stand with me and tell Mama the truth? She would have to believe both of us," I begged.

"Hannah, what's the point? That happened years ago. It doesn't matter now. Daddy is dead. Just let it go."

I couldn't believe my ears.

"I can't just let it go, Sarah. The pain of my daddy raping me for years dominates my every thought and everything I do. I still have nightmares and flashbacks about it. I can't have a meaningful relationship because of it."

"So, what if Daddy had sex with us?"

"So what? Sarah, are you on something? This shit is not normal. You are not supposed the have sex with your father," I answered as I tried very hard not to raise my already quivering voice.

"Every family has something to deal with, so you just need to drop it and move on with your life. Please, Hannah, leave it alone."

I felt like such a fool for even being there. Sarah was in my face insisting I forget about the most heinous thing that had ever happened to me; happened to us. It was like being raped again. So, I did myself a huge favor and left.

"Why did the death of your stepfather inspire you to come forth with the truth? Why not tell your mother while he was still alive," Jessica asked, "when he could have been confronted or even prosecuted?"

"I don't know. Maybe I thought it would be safer or maybe it was the ocean of accolades my stepfather was getting that sent me over the edge. Hard to say. But I wanted to let those people know the type of man he really was."

"But you didn't tell people. You only told your mother when the two of you were alone."

"Yes, so."

"Have you spoken to your mother since the funeral?"

"Barely. Maybe once or twice. Birthdays, Mother's Day, Christmas, and such.

"Has either one of you mentioned the incest again?"

"Nope."

"Hannah, you said that your mother's first reaction was disbelief. Was there something else?"

"Oh yeah, she also said I was not going to make what happened *between* my stepfather and me her fault."

"Between?"

"Yep. It's almost like she believes that it was something that I encouraged. Like we were lovers. Can you believe that?"

My eyes burned and watered at these brutal memories.

Jessica didn't say another word for a while. She just watched me and listened.

"What do you want, Hannah?" she finally asked.

"Um, I don't understand the question," I responded, a little confused and a lot offended.

"It is not a difficult question. What do you want?"

"I want my mother to believe me and to…"

"Feel sorry for you or pity you or be angry with her dead husband?"

"Yeah. Something. Anything."

"This is about you, not your mother. It is not even about your stepfather."

"What?"

Jessica softly put her pad down on the desk and slowly came to occupy the chair next to me.

"Hannah, have you forgiven your stepfather?"

"No, of course not. Why would I do that?"

"Because that's the first step you need to take toward your healing."

I felt an all-consuming firewall of anger begin to swell inside and burn the tears that streamed down my face. I could no longer remain calm or coherent.

Forgiveness?

"Forgive the man who stole my childhood? You must be

insane! Is this your professional advice? Is this what I'm paying you to tell me?" I stood and reached for my purse. I didn't know whether to pick it up and leave or to pull out my blade and stab this heifer in her face.

Forgive this shankin' since you're so into it! Forgiveness my ass! "Hannah, please. I need you to breathe and listen very carefully to what I am about to share with you."

Jessica's soft voice was more demanding now as she stood in front of me.

You need to get out of my face!

"I need to go now," I pleaded.

"You have to forgive your father. Not for him. He is dead, and nothing can be said or done that will punish him now. You have to forgive him for you. Your unforgiveness is keeping you emotionally stunted, holding you hostage. What happened to you as a child was not your fault. Neither was it your mother's fault. If she truly knew about it and failed to protect you, well she'll have to deal with it. Actually, her response to it reveals so much about the amount of pain in her it is heartbreaking. You were a child. You were not responsible for the choices the adults in your life made. Your parents failed you. But you have control over what you do and the choices you make for your life as a grown woman."

I knew she was right. I sat back down and really began to try to digest Jessica's advice.

"You see, my brother molested me for sixteen years," she revealed.

My eyes widened at her candid admission.
"I'm so sor-," I started before Jessica interrupted with a wave of

her hand.

"I know what it is like to live a life of emotional turmoil and not knowing what to do about it. Like you, I suffered in silence and allowed what happened to me to color my view of the world. I destroyed every relationship I was involved in and tried to destroy myself by experimenting with drugs, abusing my body, and even attempting suicide. I learned the hard way that the only way to get healed, I mean truly healed, was to let go and let God. Once you totally surrender your pain to Him, you will begin to experience a whole new world waiting for you to grab it with both hands."

At first, I was pissed that Jessica was preaching a sermonette. After all, she was my therapist, not my priest. But the more I listened, I mean really allowed myself to open up to what she shared I began to sense a settling presence in the room and in my spirit. It was as if the scent of the air changed around me. The tears started to spill from my eyes one at a time, then poured down my face like summer rain. My breathing became heavy as my mouth quietly whispered God's name over and over again. "Hannah don't be silent about your hurt any longer. There is no one here but you, God, and me. It's okay to let it all out. He's been waiting to help you."

I slid from the chair to my knees. From a place deep inside of me that had been dark and musty for years came sobs, moans, and finally gut-wrenching screams as sorrow escaped my soul and dissipated into mid-air. I wrapped my arms around my trembling body and held on tightly as I grieved for my lost childhood.

"Oh God, help me! I can't do this by myself anymore. I need you. Please forgive me for not trusting you to help me."

"Yes," Jessica uttered.
The moment I began to surrender the load that I'd carried

for decades, I felt lighter. Not completely weightless. Just lighter. I opened my eyes and saw Jessica's teary eyes staring back at me.

"How do you feel?"

"Worthy."

"You certainly are," Jessica answered, smiling. "There is just one more thing I'd like us to do today. I want to pray with you before you leave."

Pray?

"Okay."

I closed my eyes and bowed my head. Just then, Jessica asked if she could touch me.

"Sure," I answered, reaching out my hands. Instead, she wrapped her arms around me in a tight embrace.

"Dear Heavenly Father," she began.

Dr. Bryce's prayer was powerful. No one had ever prayed just for me like that before. Not even my own mother. My heart was full of so many things at that moment, I thought it might explode.

This is what has been waiting for me? I will not allow myself to suffer anymore. I will not suffer.

"Amen," she concluded.

"Amen," I agreed.

We both exhaled and I once again saw Jessica's patient smile break through her own tears.

"Okay, Miss Hannah. You have taken an important step to becoming a well-healed woman; however, there is more work you must do. See you next week."

"I'm ready."

I'm so ready for this.

The smile on my face was real for the first time in a very long time. My days of suffering in silence were over. I had a choice in how I lived, and I wanted to live free. The journey wouldn't be easy, but it would be well worth the work.

Let's go, Hannah!

Meet Tracy M. Dorsey

Author and storyteller, Tracy M. Dorsey (former pen, Hazel Mills), knew she wanted to be a writer from the time she penned her first poem in third grade.

Tracy has written three novels and published numerous short stories and articles. Her first book, Bare Necessities: Sensuous Tales of Passion, was nominated for an African American Literary Award in 2008 and was voted Best Erotic Fiction by African Americans on the Move Book Club in 2009.

Tracy was included in Who's Who in Black Birmingham in 2009 and in Who's Who in Black Alabama in 2014. Tracy lives in Birmingham with her husband of 30 years and her three sons. She writes and performs inspirational poetry for her church and for the NAACP's Women's History Month events.

The Purpose in Your Pain
Carla Victoria Wallace

Does your pain have a purpose?
Is there a reason for it all?
Is it to make you stronger?
Or is it to make you fall?
The enemy will try to deceive you,
Make you think you were a forgotten mistake.
But God said He will never leave you,
Your burdens He will take
So, don't call it your pain,
Call it your purpose.
When you give God your pain,
You can watch Him work it,
Together for the good;
You'll do things
You thought you never could.
In a sea of forgiveness,
You will be washed;
Pass that forgiveness to others.
Sins of the past will be squashed,
Buried, no longer can it control you.
Pain no longer follows you,
Purpose you will step into,
Transformed into someone new.
Sarai became Sarah,
Which means bitterness turned to laughter,
God made her an older mother.
Soon after Abram became Abraham,
A father of many, even in old age,
Offspring a plenty.
Jesus became The Christ,
Crucified on Earth,
Resurrected the third day,
To give us new birth.

Saul became Paul,
Transformed from his past,
A persecutor of Christians,
The truth made him free at last.
Araminta Ross became Harriet Tubman,
A runaway slave made free;
She refused to settle for,
What others told her she had to be.
So, who will you become on purpose?

Some of the people mentioned in this poem are from Bible stories I grew up hearing as a child in Sunday School. Maybe you consider yourself a Christian, maybe you don't. Maybe you grew up in church, maybe you didn't. Either way, if you take the time to listen to the message in this poem and in the stories mentioned, there is a common theme. Any 3333pain you are experiencing now does not have to defeat you or destroy you. If you hold on and give that pain to God, he can bring you out in a way you could have never imagined.

I grew up having an identity crisis. Years later, I wrote a fictional book called "The Ultimate Love," inspired by that crisis and by the things I had seen during that crisis, which opened the door to my becoming an author. I will give you a little background about that crisis.

I was born and raised in a diverse town that had a variety of different cultures. Some of my best friends as a child had Asian American backgrounds, and another good childhood friend of mine was white. We learned from one another, accepted one another, and were happy. Due to interracial marriages in my family, I also had an Asian American aunt, and a white aunt.

Coming from an African American background, my parents taught me about my culture and that we were the descendants of slaves. We were proud of how our family had overcome those setbacks. My father's parents were able to build a house on the same land in the South that they had once picked cotton on. My dad was one of the first children to integrate schools in the southern town he grew up in. My mother's parents became self-employed and were able to leave the South and buy a house in southern Connecticut so that my mother and her siblings would not have to attend segregated schools. My father joined the Navy and became a hospital corpsman. My mother was a first-generation college graduate from the University of Connecticut and became an administrative supervisor. They let me know that achieving as a black person could be harder because of discrimination.

When I was eight years old, my family and I joined a predominately African American church and began to develop new friendships. When I was nine years old, my parents made the decision to send me to a prestigious school which was located in an affluent white community. It was navigating both of those environments which led to my question, "Where do I fit in?" I did not relate to the backgrounds of many of the students in my school. Then when I began hanging out with friends from church, they started asking me questions like, "Why do you talk like a white girl?" I did not realize at the time that attending school in an affluent white community had begun to change parts of my personality.

That same year, my teacher at that school assigned us a family project describing where we are from. My parents let me know that as descendants of slaves, we could not trace what actual country in Africa we may have been from, and Ancestry DNA kits did not exist at that time. So, my dad helped me make a plantation to describe where my family was from. We recounted our painful family history by building a miniature "big house" surrounded by smaller "slave quarters" made of toothpicks, obviously not nearly as nice as the "big house" in the center. I was the only child at the time who brought in a plantation, while other students knew what countries their families originated from, but I understood that it was my history. My parents did not shelter me from that history and let me watch the movie, "Roots" around that time as well. However, seeing the obvious difference in me, I was often treated differently by my peers at the school I was attending. I began to feel misunderstood, and I did not like it.

For high school, my parents took me out of the school, and I attended my local high school. It was more of the diverse setting I was used to in my early childhood years. I interacted with black, white, and Hispanic students throughout my time in high school; however, most of my close friends were black at that time. Inside, I was still struggling with parts of my identity and trying to figure out who I was and where I fit in. That struggle led to me making choices that did not reflect who, deep down, I knew God wanted me to be. I almost lost myself completely, headed down a troubling path.

After high school, I began to find myself slowly. I followed in my mother's footsteps and attended the University of Connecticut. I participated in activities at the African American Cultural Center. I began establishing diverse friendships again. New friends invited me to Latin American events, where we danced to Latin American music. I became comfortable in my skin as an African American woman who enjoys getting to know people from various ethnic backgrounds. God has created us all uniquely different, and all are welcome in God's family. If we celebrate our diversity, embrace, and understand one another. How much better could things be?

After college, I began teaching in a diverse school district, and I realized that my background had indeed prepared me for that role in which I would interact with families from Hispanic, white, black, and Asian backgrounds. I married my husband and blended into their family, who had immigrated from Jamaica. My husband and I joined a multicultural non-denominational church full of many cultures, with branches across the globe.

In a previous anthology, "A Mother's Love" I shared a bit of my painful struggles to become a mother. We now have three daughters who attend one of the most diverse schools in the state.

I became the author of ethnically diverse books for adults and children. Parents from all backgrounds purchase my children's books. I have had black and Hispanic parents tell me that it is so good to see books with characters their children can relate to. My pain as a child and adolescent experiencing an identity crisis turned into purpose through the words and books that I wrote. In 2021 I was selected to be one of the equity leaders in my school district, which I believe my past background has prepared me for.

I also realized that, beyond race or ethnicity, my most important identity is as a child of God. "The most important part of our identities is who God has created us to be and who he has called us to be." If we let Him, God will take all parts of who we are and our past experiences and turn them into a masterpiece. So, I leave you again with this question, "Who will you become, on purpose?"

Meet Carla Victoria Wallace

Carla Victoria Wallace graduated from the University of Connecticut where she majored in elementary education with a concentration in English. She then became an elementary school teacher by day, and author by night.

She is the author of two fiction novels titled, The Ultimate Love and Love Connection, and three children's books titled The Bug That Was Afraid of the Dark, The Bug That Went On The Field Trip, and Little Miracle. In 2018, her book, The Bug That Was Afraid Of The Dark, won "Best Children's Book" at the "African American Literary Awards Show" in New York City.

In addition to being a teacher and author, Carla enjoys her roles of being a wife and mother to her husband and three young daughters.

The Journey for Love
Cee Cee H. Caldwell

Hello Queens, I pray that all is well with you. I understand that life has been hard for many and so many things are happening and sometimes it is hard to make it through the tough times. I want to encourage you all that you can make it through just hold on to God's unchanging hands and keep the faith. No matter what comes your way, I have faith enough to believe that you will come through.

I want to share just a little bit of my story to let you know that it doesn't matter how you start, but what is important is how you finish. Well, here goes. I was born in Washington DC on August 29, 1968, at DC General Hospital by a single mother, and that may not sound hard, but here is the challenging, painful part. I was born a product of rape, so I am a rape baby. Yeah, I said it. It wasn't always easy for me to say because I did not know that until I was very much older, and as you can imagine, it devastated me to my core. This has not been an easy thing to take over my life for many reasons.

For one, not having a father in my life has always caused me some grief because I just wanted to have Daddy's' love and that was not the path chosen. I would look at my friends with their fathers as well as the other little girls with their dads and would daydream what it would be like if I had someone to love me, protect me, and make me feel special every day of my life.
I was blessed with my godfather, who was there as much as he could be, but let's face it, he was not my dad, and he had a family of his own. Besides, he knew he was not my dad, but I believed that he was until I found out he wasn't when I was 14, which was another blow to the gut. I was so broken that words could not express how I was feeling. Here I go again feeling unwanted, unloved, and not enough.
Now I know it wasn't my godfather's fault and I

wondered why I was led to believe a lie for so long. You see, parents make choices and decisions that they say are in the best interest of their children when the truth is, they are doing what is best for themselves. What was a little black girl in Washington, D.C., to do? My mother did the best she could to raise her three children on her own. I was the youngest and the only girl. I had to grow up quickly because I forgot to mention that my mother was sick, so I had to step in and help in any way that I knew how. I had to become a homemaker as a kid; I cooked, cleaned, and did whatever I needed to make sure when my mom came home from work, all she had to do was eat and rest and that was pretty much the routine.

She worked to keep a roof over our heads; however, we moved frequently but she kept us together. It was not always easy not knowing where we were going to live, or what we were going to eat, but Mom always made a way somehow. Being the only daughter, I felt that it was my responsibility to do whatever I had to, even though I had two older brothers in the mix, it seems that specific responsibilities fall on the female child. I have no idea, but it just is what it is. I still felt like I had no choice but to fill those roles early on in my life. Did I mention nobody asked me if I wanted to do these things? It was just expected.

Can you imagine how a little girl in Washington, D.C., must have felt when she saw her mother in an ambulance with those bright lights and loud-sounding sirens repeatedly going from hospital to hospital and not knowing what to do, what they were doing to her, and if she was going to come home? It was painful, scary, and sometimes too much to bear. Some of you may have never experienced this, and some of you have, and if you have, you never get used to it. You just adapt. I had no choice but to manage to get through it, and even at a young age, I needed an escape.

During those times, I still desired and longed to be loved and I yearned for it so deeply. You see, my family wasn't the loving type of family expressively if you understand what I mean. And maybe you don't because you were raised with two loving parents who set an example of what unconditional love looked and you saw it exhibited daily. If that was your deal, I am so happy for you, and I know you realized how blessed you were, if they are living, how fortunate you truly are.

My mother did not know how to express love so much because she had her own issues, and she was really a loner. You didn't see her with a lot of people, and we did not have a lot of people visiting our home, adults anyway. She stayed to herself most of the time, and I was the complete opposite. I loved being with people and having friends throughout my life. My house was the house that the kids came to, and she made everyone feel like they mattered. They would call her "mom," and I said to myself, if they were calling her that, then I expect them to treat her like that. Well, some did, and some didn't, I know you know how that goes.

When it came to her children, she showed her love by meeting our needs and making sure we had a roof over our heads, food to eat, and clothes on our backs as best as she could. Of course, I was grateful. She also made sure we were spiritually rooted and grounded. Did I mention I was a church baby? My siblings and I have been in church all our lives. I used to do homework in the back and fell asleep on the pews. When the church was open, we were there unless she wasn't feeling her best, but even then, Mom pressed her way. She gave us the best gift that anyone could ever receive, and that is the example of unconditional love, the love of Jesus Christ. So, I had known Jesus at a young age, and I loved him, and he loved me back. More on that a little later…

However, there was still an emptiness inside of me that could not seem to be filled at all. It is unexplainable. If you have not had that experience of feeling like there is a deep, dark, black hole that is inside of you, and you just want it filled. You desire to feel whole, and you just simply feel broken and shattered. Remember, I am a rape baby and those thoughts have plagued me all my life. How does a child reconcile that? And I am a daddy-less daughter who must watch day in and day out what she dreams about, what she longs for, what she desires, but can't have for obvious reasons and that is fathers loving their daughters by having daddy-daughter dates, dances, and just daddy-daughter time. I felt like every time I saw it, I lost a piece of me. That didn't stop me from seeking to be loved by someone, anyone who would be willing to make me feel special, loved, and valued.

You see, due to me not feeling pretty enough, good enough, smart enough, wanted enough, or just plain enough, I began to feel like I had to please people. I did what was asked of me even if I didn't want to because I did not want people to walk out on me and leave me with the scars of abandonment once again. I believe some knew it and took my kindness for weakness, but truthfully, I allowed it because I wanted whatever they were willing to be and do in my life for however long it was to last. Can you imagine just wanting to be loved so badly that you accepted anything from anyone? You know this was a temporary fix to an even deeper problem.

As far as I was concerned, I had no identity. I didn't know my father for obvious reasons so then I had to settle for being included in anyone's life for as long as they would allow me to, how fun was that if you can imagine. Now I am not saying that the people in my life were not genuine or just users because all of them were not some of them loved me as they knew how, and I knew it others wanted what they could get for as long as they could get it. But I take full responsibility for all things today, I don't point fingers, make excuses, or offer scapegoats for what I have experienced in my life.

I was always involved in activities coming up as a kid into my adult life and I was good at certain things, but I still doubted myself a lot. But no matter how I felt I still did not have a complete identity, so I had to create one. I had to face the fact that I would never know my father or his family so what it caused me to do was to love the way I desired to be loved, and truthfully, that was a hard pill to swallow at times because the love I gave was not the love I received most of the time.

I am a loyalist if I love you, I love with all that I am, every beat of my heart bleeds for you when you are in pain, I feel that is how I love and even if you don't return it the way I need, I had a habit of just taking what you gave me. Now notice I said 'had.' I have learned my value over the years and no longer settle for lopsided love or love that is not mutually benefiting because I have come to a place to understand what true unadulterated or tainted love looks like. It took me a long while to understand that I deserved to be loved in a way that did not hurt me, demean me, or make me feel worthless in any way whatsoever.

My first boyfriend while I was in Washington D.C. was named Dexter and he was so sweet, and kind. He would write me poetry in cards, and believe it or not, I kept them until a few years ago, and I still have a picture of him and I together. Now I know some of you would say that was puppy love but remember I would take love how I could get it. We were kids but there is something about the love of children that is so innocent, pure, and fulfilling. What I thought was love from Dexter was really what I call baby love and it was special, and even when I think of him and it today, it still makes me smile. If only adult love could be as kind, sweet, gentle, and pure as baby love. I know it can, it just takes work and a mutual heart for one another.

So, see with Dexter is where my journey for love really began, I knew he loved me as sweetly as he could, we were young. But due to my mom's illness, we relocated to New Jersey when I was 12 years old, so I had to leave Dexter and the love we shared. It was sweet, innocent but special and as you see, I still remember it today. It may be no big deal by other people's standard, but it was to me.

So, as I prepared to say goodbye and move to New Jersey and start a new chapter of my life, feelings of uncertainty, abandonment, unworthiness took over me. I had no choice but to move, I was 12 years old; I had to go, and I wondered would I find love from anyone else again. We shall see is what I said to myself. So off to the Garden State for a new beginning, a fresh start, and a new identity.

Jersey bound I was, and I didn't meet anyone of interest right away. Let's face it, I was in middle school for just a few months and then on to high school it was. I was the new girl on the block, a stranger in a new state, town, and city. I wasn't really interested in anyone for a while, I was just concerned about school and my after-school activities, which was a good thing. There was someone that caught my eye, but he had a girlfriend, so I just had a silent crush for a long time and moved on.

In the meantime, I still wanted to be loved and the older I got the more that I seemed to crave it like it was a drug that I was addicted to. During my high school years, I met some nice guys and some users but that was my fault because my way of choosing was not calculated, it was surface choosing. Is he fine? Does he say I am beautiful? Is he showing me kindness? That is not so bad, but when you are young and attracted to older men because you are still yearning the love of a father, and they somehow can tell you are desperate for love, they play along with you. They told me what I wanted to hear, acted like they cared. I am not saying all of them, but let's face it, I was a pretty young thing, light skinned with big thighs and breast to match. I was affectionate, friendly, and willing to give all that I had. Remember I did say I was loyal and a people pleaser. My body was an attention getter, and I knew it because I was physically mature. I just didn't realize that the attention I got was not the kind I wanted to get but some attention was better than no attention, right? Wrong.

I was a church girl that had a lot of inner turmoil going on and I could put on a brave face and make everyone feel special but me because, if you didn't know, I have been acting since I was 5 years old. I have always wanted to become a professional actress, but life had other plans for me. I know how to be someone else really well.

Being raised in church did not come without its pain and hurt. I was raped at 16 by a member of the church and that changed me for life. I remember it like it was yesterday. I used to take my dance teacher's daughter to school, you see, and she would pick me up every day, and take me to her daughter's school. I would wait until she went to class, and I would walk to Clifford J. Scott High School, which was not too far, and I was always on time for my classes. So, this particular morning my mother was leaving for work, and she yelled, "I am leaving," and I continued getting ready for school and prepared to be picked up as I would on a usual day. This day would not be usual at all, and it would change me forever.

I was in my room in the attic putting on a teal and black sweat suit when I heard someone coming up the stairs and was startled because I did not know that there was a member of my church watching the kids downstairs. Some of what happened gets blurry and I guess that is just my defense mechanism kicking in. All I remember is being thrown on the bed with a knife at my throat. I begged him to stop as I told him that my teacher would be waiting for me while praying that she would come knock on the door, but she never did, or I didn't hear her. He didn't care at all, he saw what he wanted, and he was going to get it at all costs. So, he wouldn't kill me I let him do what he came to do, and he threatened me, of course, that I would be hurt if I told anyone. Once he satisfied his itch in the way he desired, he got up and went back downstairs as if nothing happened.

Now rape is about power because sex, you can get from

anyone, even if you have to pay for it, you. Most rapists have unresolved mommy issues or psychological ones. Frankly, it didn't matter to me what his issues were, I knew that my life would never be the same.

At the time of my rape, I was dating a devil worshipper because I knew it would drive my mother nuts. I was rebellious and still upset that I was daddy-less and lied to about who my father was for so long because I thought it was my godfather until I was told differently at 14-years-old.

Back to the rape story. I was mad at him, my mom, church leadership, others, God, and myself. I did not understand why something so devastating and violent had to happen to me and what had I done to deserve this, but it did. I was in a state of complete shock, and I remember the counselor telling my mother that she had better keep an eye on me because I had not responded in the manner in which she thought I would. I had a tendency to hold onto my feelings and try to please others and make them happy.

I called one of my best male friends and asked him where he was, and he told me, and I met him at the clinic where he was taking his son to. I told him what happened and of course he consoled me, and I went home with him. He called my boyfriend (yes the devil worshipper) and told him what happened, and he absolutely lost it, and then we finally called my mother. She came and picked me up and I was taken to East Orange General Hospital to have a rape kit done.

If you have never experienced this, you will never know that being violated continues. The swabbing for fluids, and I had not removed the clothes that I was wearing so, they tried to find evidence, and on top that having to spread my legs open for strangers review me like I was a medical project was not cool at all, but of course I did what I always did. I let them do what they had to do. Then the questions and after all those questions, we headed to the police station.

When I got to the police station, of course there were more questions, and you would not believe that my rapist was sitting in my uncle, pastor Apostle's house like nothing happened. Yes, my mom called and told him what happened. She told the police where he was as well. And if things could not get any worse for me this day, imagine being told by your mother not to press charges because here is some truth… I was not a virgin, and her thought was, if I went to trial, they would abuse me with that information, and so trusting my mother, the woman who gave me life, I did not press charges. But he was supposed to stay away from me, but as far as I can remember, I did not have to press charges against him, the state was going to do it. I was devastated already, but to have my mother tell me not to press charges was too much for me to handle.

That night my boyfriend got arrested because, after he found out what happened to me, he snapped and ended up in a jail cell. My mother went to speak with him, and they did release him, and she showed up at my house with him. I was in a catatonic state and talked with him and told him that we could not be together anymore. I felt like garbage and that no one would want me after this so I let him go before he could hurt me.

Another cycle of my life began but we will talk about that in a few. So just a recap, born a rape baby, the father I have known emotionally stolen from me at 14, and at 16 raped by a church member and then I was forced to go back to church and who do I see? You got it, I was seeing my rapist. What do you think happened to me? How do you think that made me feel? How do you think I responded? I became even more rebellious, I drank to ease the pain, and I became desperate to be loved even more which I know may sound crazy because it did to me. Somewhere in my mind I felt that if a man wanted me, it would just be best to give up myself than for it to be taken from me violently because it may cost me my life.

There is something that happens to your soul when you are violated in such a manner. I always handled my business, whether I was working, going to school, or whatever I put my mind to, I accomplished. At the same time, I found comfort in the arms of man and a bottle. I thought I was in control when really, they were getting what they wanted without a real commitment, and I took what I could get because I felt that was what I deserved. That behavior went on for years until I truly recommitted my life to Jesus Christ. I got saved when I was a child, but I became sold out for Jesus as an adult. I was tired of being hurt, abused, used, and taken for granted. However, I had to take full responsibility for the choices that I made and own them all.

After all of that I thought that I found the man that I would spend the rest of my life with, and guess where I met him? You guessed it, at the church. He was a minister and organist, and I was the choir directress at my church. Yes, I stayed at the church where I was abused, that is a whole different story. He was kind, I just saw him as a brother because I was in a 2-year relationship when I met him. That relationship ended because I woke up and realized then if a man says he loves you and it is real, he must show it because love is not what it says, it is what it does. So long story short, I ended the relationship I was in and started dating the pastor organist that paid attention.

We started dating in April 1997, got engaged May 24, 1997, and were married October 18, 1997. Yeah, I know, I did not have time to heal but I didn't think I needed to because he treated me the way I wanted to be treated. Oh, did I mention he has two pre-teens from his 1st marriage? And yes, I loved him; he was chocolate and fine and I was caramel and fly and we made the perfect match. Well, at least I thought so. Jump ahead 20 years and there is a lot to say about that, but this is not the space for it. Who I thought I would be with forever became the man that I would divorce on September 28, 2017. I think because of abandonment and unproven infidelity, and I say I think because truthfully, I didn't want the divorce, he did. After crying out before God in a Motel 6 Room 279 day in and day out literally dying on the inside not understanding how the man I gave everything to, even my identity, could just leave me abandoned in a motel to fend for myself. Now he took care of the room most of the time. I ended up getting a job at Marshall's so that I could provide for myself making $9.00 an hour and let me tell you this: I have 4 degrees and yes, I worked for $9.00 an hour. It may not seem like much, but it helped me begin to put the pieces of my life back together, learn how to love me as God loved me and simply how to live again on my own.

Believe it or not, I can tell anyone how to divorce and do it with style and class and that is another subject for another day. I did it my way and then I decided that I needed a fresh start and time to heal for real this time. I needed to heal from being a rape baby, daddy-less and a divorced pastor's wife so that I could have the love that Jesus Christ has for me. Do you want to know how I survived all of this? It is quite easy and simple; I shifted my focus off of man and the world and focused on being the Queen that God created me to be.

I had been depressed for years, I have thought of taking my own life for years, I have thought negative thoughts about myself for years, and I have still on occasion, sought the approval of others to be validated until I really dug deep into God and his Word which tells me, and you, that we are fearfully and wonderfully made as God's Masterpiece. You and I are joint heirs with Christ if we accept him as our Lord and Savior. I started my life over in Georgia at almost 50 years old and I thought many of days that I would not make it, if it had not been for Almighty God in Heaven who is my example of ultimate unconditional love. Otherwise, I would not be here today. Queens let me leave you with this; learn to love yourself the way that God loves you, and when you do, you will not SETTLE for any love that is not the godly love you were Created and Chosen by God to receive. You are a God Designed Lady who is LOVED.

I will leave you with this Apology letter I wrote to myself. You may want to give it a try, you will be amazed at how freeing this can be. I love you all and there's nothing you can do about it, and if you need me, you know where to find me on FB. "Be real, be true, be authentic and be you because you are more than enough."

My Apology Letter to Me…
Dear Cee Cee,

I apologize for playing small all these years after being laid off twice and connecting your value and worth to your jobs. You know what God told you to do and He has equipped you with everything needed to fulfill His plan for your life. I am sorry for putting everyone else's needs before yours. I am sorry for championing everyone else but you. I apologize for allowing depression, doubt, and scarcity to consume you over the past 20+ years. I am sorry for half stepping and looking for validation from others and not God alone. I am sorry for letting you become a doormat to many under the disguise of being a servant of the Lord. I am sorry for allowing the role of Pastor's wife make you feel inferior to others and cause you to isolate yourself from your true identity as a woman. I apologize for not connecting to those you were assigned to strengthen and support. I am sorry for not being everything that you knew you were supposed to be because I allowed what others thought, said, or did consume me. I know that God has great things in store you and you will no longer continue to put yourself on the bottom of your own priority list. You will show up every day for you, being the Kingdom Woman God masterfully designed you to be on purpose with intention. You will do what you must, and it starts now because the longer you take the more people will be affected by your absence in their lives. You are more than enough, and you have everything you need to live the abundant and authentic life that God desires for you. You must know that from this moment on, you must rise up and be the light the world is waiting for, the authentic you, to show up and so am I. Forgive yourself for not maximizing this precious gift called TIME. You will now play full out and you will never quit until your assignment has been complete and God will say, "Well done, thy Good and Faithful Servant."

I love you with everything I am, and you were designed and destined for greatness. I will see you at the top because the bottom is way too crowded. It is time for you to rise up like the phoenix from the ashes and soar like the eagle.
No more apologies are necessary because you are going to start living your best life NOW!!

Love Your Authentic Self
Cee The Lady

Meet Cee Cee H. Caldwell

Transformational Thought Leader/Self-Care Sensei, Kingdom Wellness Ambassador, Authenticity Advocate, SYMBIS Facilitator Practitioner/International Best-Selling Author/Beauty, Style and Wellness Entrepreneur, Licensed Evangelist

Cee Cee resides in Ellenwood Georgia. She attended Trenton State College, where she received a BA in Communication with a minor in African American Studies. Her love for helping people caused her to pursue an MA in Counseling, Human Services and Guidance from Montclair State University. Cee Cee believes in continual education no matter what because applied knowledge is potential power.

Cee Cee has had a love for writing since she was 5 years old. Cee Cee believes that everyone has a story to tell. Her love for the written word has increased over the years. In 2008, Cee Cee released her 1st book called Be In Good Health: Living a Life of Happiness, Wholeness and Wellness which endeavors to help people live their best life, from the inside out. Unspoken Words – "LOVE" Volume 1, released in October 2014. Stewardship and Service: God's Way or Our Way was released in Winter 2016 through Imani Faith Publishing.

Cee Cee has written for the following magazines/newspapers:
Examiner – Central Jersey Holistic Health (2011)
Real Life Real Faith Women Walking by Faith (Senior Managing Editor) (2015)
Real Life Real Faith Journey to Wellness (2015)
Identity Magazine (2016) and so many more.

Cee Cee is a member of Sigma Gamma Rho Sorority, Inc., the Real Sisters Rising Women's Business Association, Women Speakers Association, Non-Fiction Writers Association, and other organizations/associations. Cee Cee believes that "You must

READ to SUCCEED, because readers are leaders!" Through her speaking, workshops and books her desire is to *Encourage, Enlighten and Empower* others *to walk in their Greatness by living an Authentic and Intentional Life ON PURPOSE as Designed by GOD!*

Saving My Life, NOT My Image
Rashidah Id-Deen

My name is Rashidah Id-Deen and I'm a multiple Survivor of Rape/Sexual Assaults and domestic violence. My first experience and journey of rape/sexual abuse began at the tender age of 12 yrs. old. It was that horrific, devastating experience, which robbed Me of my virginity and stole my innocence and purity. Little did I know that violence experience, would become the catalyst that would change my Life FOREVER.

Consequently, the trajectory of my Life, from that point forward would continue to be filled with additional rapes AND domestic violence abuse. This resulted in my entire sense of SELF-Worth, SELF-esteem, SELF-awareness; bottom line my whole sense of SELF identity, was TOTALLY obliterated.
It was the last sexual assault, by a professional, well-known massage/rehabilitation specialist. That I eventually found my voice and my willingness and determination to speak UP, speak OUT and FIGHT on behalf of MYSELF. I took the sexual abuser to court/trial. And WON! He was convicted as a sexual felon, sentenced to 7 years prison time. And lifetime monitoring subjective to "Meagan Law." Which must notify the community/area upon his release. That a convicted sexual felon resides within their community/neighborhood.

However, this WIN would be short-lived. The convicted sexual felon filed an appeal, based on a "juror technicality" and won. The caveat to this was, if I chose NOT to take him to trial, a second time. Not only would he be released. But additionally, he would no longer have a convicted sexual felon record.

So, when the Prosecutor's Office, informed Me of this. I LITERALLY felt sick to my stomach. To think after a grueling, life-changing sexual assault trial. It would be ALL for naught. Was EXTREMELY devastating. The Prosecutor gingerly informed Me that, they would COMPLETELY understand if I didn't want to go through another grueling trial. However, it took Me all of (2) minutes to say to the Prosecutor. I'm IN! If I did nothing else but hurt him in his pockets, at least he would know, I NEVER gave IN nor UP! So, let's get ready to RUMBLE!!

Now, during the second trial, the jurors were not allowed to know that this was a second trial. However, the Judge, along with the Prosecutor and myself, were aware that this was a second trial. About halfway through the second trial. His attorney sensed that WE were gonna get a conviction. And in the event that We did. His sentence would start anew. ALL over again. And the year sentence served thus far.. Would be null and void.

Surprisingly, his attorney convinced him to plead guilty. Whereby his sentence would run concurrently with his time already served. And not risk the possibility of being sentenced with more than the initial 7 yrs. imposed during the first trial.

Upon pleading guilty, the Judge informed him that he would NOT have any further appeal options. And at this point, the jury became aware that this was his second trial.

The hugest and BEST take away I received from these entire overwhelming trials was this. NO ONE can SAVE Us, nor HEAL Us; but US. The image facade, I had developed out of survival mode. Did NOT protect Me; but weakened Me. Establishing and finding my VOICE, my identity and authenticity, was GOD'S Healing Mercy and Grace for and upon Me. I'm FOREVER Grate-FULL to have learned to; "Save My Life; NOT My Image."

Now, let me take you back, on a journey in time. On a day that would change my Life, FOREVER. Which became the impetus for a lifetime of shame, guilt, fear, secrecy, and complete annihilation of who I was; and who I may have become. Manifested in Me, a NEED, to create an IMAGE, in my mind which was more acceptable. And more relatable and palatable. Then the jaded reality of what was NOW my Life. Hijacking my individual authenticity.

"Innocent, But No Longer Pure."

I remember being excited on that Monday, July 11th. It was my Father's Birthday. I was 12 yrs. old. It was a joyous day. I could now finally use the money that I earned from summer babysitting to buy him a gift. That was a proud moment for Me. The weather forecast was for a high of 95 degrees. I remember waking up early that morning and rushing to my closet to check out the fashionable dressed skirts and blouses crowding my closet. I pictured the stylish models in Ebony Magazine. That special day, I would do my best to look just like one of them.

I had a lot of frilly, very feminine clothes, that I always accessorized with bows and whatnot. But there was this particular dress I wore all the time (smiles) because it my favorite. I felt so grown up in it.
The dress was brown and beige. All nice and soft with a cotton feel to it. When I wore it I would spin around in a circle and my dress twirled with Me. It made Me look like a young Woman, not a child.

That morning when my mother came into my room. I was already dressed and spinning. Rashidah, why ALWAYS that dress? Mama sometimes had a unique way of frowning and smiling at the same time. It makes me feel all grown up, I beamed.

She shook her head. Mama loved seeing me happy but hated seeing her little girl grow up so fast. She knew what I did not, yet. The world could be awful cold and cruel for a Woman. But maybe, just maybe she could spare her baby girl, at least for a while.

Rashidah! Stop trying to grow up so fast! I managed to stop twirling under Mama's watchful eye. Besides, there were other fun things I could do.

I delighted in experimenting with new hairstyles and fashion trends, like those in magazines. It would drive my parents crazy. Daddy would have been happy with me in braids ribbons and bows, forever. Which is how my Grandma Eula always styled my hair.

I also reveled in listening to music mature music. Jazz and R&B were staples in our household. As so were books.

Fantasizing was another fun thing I liked to do. I loved imagining myself as a future Woman, wife, and Mother. I wanted to be the best, as all three.

I was both a little girl and a budding young Woman. Music, books, fashion, and fantasies transported me into a realm of grown-up consciousness. A grown-up World, with feelings that were foreign to the child in me; yet intriguing.

Finally, it was time for me to go babysit. I almost ran down the street to the children's apartment, by myself. Back then in the 60's, growing up there were no worries about people abducting children. It was a safe place to be growing up; so, I thought in Newark, NJ.

The babies were napping in their bedroom, I had fed them. So far so good. My parents would have been proud of me. I was proud of me. It was time for a little reward.

Remember, music was an important part of my life. I put a 45 black vinyl record on the turntable in the living room. It played 33s, 45s, and 78s. Remember them?
The record on the turntable was my favorite. "Face It Girl; It's

Over." By the fabulous Ms. Nancy Wilson. It was number fifteen on the US R&B chart.

I was singing in the bathroom, restyling my hair for the nth time. And beaming at my reflection in the mirror. I was in a picture-perfect little world. The calm before the storm.
He came home early. The children's father called out for me from the living room. Rashidah!

Hi! My voice must have sounded so young and innocent. I wasn't expecting you home so soon I said. Is anything wrong? He was sitting on the sofa. He patted a space on it near him. I'm not feeling well, Rashidah! The children's father reached for me. Come on over here, he said. Sit next to me. His voice was authoritative. Now, I was raised to mind my elders. I thought nothing of following his orders. Grown-ups protected you, right? He took one of my hands, guiding me to the sofa to sit beside him. You're such pretty girl. He smiled. I know now that I was staring into the face of danger. But there was no way I could presage the end of an era of my Life. An era of innocence.

This was before the proliferation of daytime talk show TV, with live interviews from rapists in prison. This was a pre-Oprah time, before home audiences viewed packaged wisdom dispensed between commercials.

Thank you, I answered. My home training demanded my politeness. What came next was beyond anything in a child's book of etiquette. His grown man's fingers started caressing and trailing up and down my arms. Though naive, I knew something was so wrong. NO! I tried to pull away but could not away from his groping hands. PLEASE... I begged, still not wanting to believe it. Of course, he just got bolder, hearing my plea.

Rashidah! He ripped my beautiful brown and beige dress off my shoulder. STOP I cried. What are you doing? A hard, clawing hand under my dress, prying open my locked legs, answered me.

I wept. The children's father was now my monster. I wondered how in heaven he could... He disgusted me. Prying open my cramping thighs, sucking on my aching, bruised breasts....

I was living a nightmare that only got worse.

I remember one moment more vividly than all others that day. The sharp, ripping pain as he stabbed my vagina with his penis. I was a virgin. He was mean and vicious. I knew then, he had planned this. I fought with all my strength. The more I fought to re-clamp my legs. The more vicious he got. Can't he tell that I'm locked? I kept thinking. I'm locked.

That human piece of filth broke my lock. Do you remember the record; "Face it Girl; It's Over." It was set to repeat. and played over and over. It was as if this song, once my favorite, was personally telling me something.

My purity was over. Innocence? Over. My mind was overwhelmed with pain, fear, and confusion. Eventually, a mental fugue spared me from what seemed like a never-ending nightmare.

I cannot tell you where the children were while the babysitter was being violated by their dad if they were still sleeping or not. Telling my parents was the next nightmare. They were devastated, angry, shocked, and ashamed. All of my Dad's birthday. What a hell of a birthday present.

On that day, July 11th. I started the day as a young girl, full of joy and hope. By the day's end. I was traumatized. And that trauma would shadow me the rest of my Life.

Meet Rashidah Id-Deen

My name is Rashidah Id-Deen and I'm a multiple Survivor of Rape/Sexual Assaults and domestic violence. My first experience and journey of rape/sexual abuse began at the tender age of 12 yrs. old. It was that horrific, devastating experience, which robbed Me of my virginity and stole my innocence and purity. Little did I know that, that violence experience, would become the catalyst that would change my Life FOREVER..

Consequently, the trajectory of my Life, from that point forward would continue to be filled with additional rapes AND domestic violence abuse. This resulted in my entire sense of SELF-Worth, SELF-esteem, SELF-awareness; bottom line my whole sense of SELF identity, was TOTALLY obliterated.

It was the last sexual assault, by a professional, well-known massage/rehabilitation specialist. That I eventually found my voice and my willingness and determination to speak UP, speak OUT and FIGHT on behalf of MYSELF. I took the sexual abuser to court/trial. And WON! He was convicted as a sexual felon, sentenced to 7 years prison time. And lifetime monitoring subjective to "Meagan Law." Which must notify the community/area upon his release. That a convicted sexual felon resides within their community/neighborhood.

However, this WIN would be short-lived. The convicted sexual felon filed an appeal, based on a "juror technicality" and won. The caveat to this was, if I chose NOT to take him to trial, a second time. Not only would he be released. But additionally, he would no longer have a convicted sexual felon record.

So, when the Prosecutor's Office, informed Me of this. I LITERALLY felt sick to my stomach. To think after a grueling, life-changing sexual assault trial. It would be ALL for naught. Was EXTREMELY devastating. The Prosecutor gingerly informed Me that, they would COMPLETELY understand if I didn't want to go through another grueling trial. However, it took Me all of (2) minutes to say to the Prosecutor. I'm IN! If I did nothing else but hurt him in his pockets, at least he would know, I NEVER gave IN nor UP! So, let's get ready to RUMBLE!!

Now, during the second trial, the jurors were not allowed to know that this was a second trial.. However, the Judge, along with the Prosecutor and myself, were aware that this was a second trial. About halfway through the second trial. His attorney sensed that WE were gonna get a conviction. And in the event that We did. His sentence would start anew. ALL over again. And the year sentence served thus far.. Would be null and void.

Surprisingly, his attorney convinced him to plead guilty. Whereby his sentence would run concurrently with his time already served. And not risk the possibility of being sentenced with more than the initial 7 years. imposed during the first trial.

Upon pleading guilty, the Judge informed him that he would NOT have any further appeal options. And at this point, the jury became aware that this was his second trial.

The hugest and BEST take away I received from these entire overwhelming trials was this. NO ONE can SAVE Us, nor HEAL Us; but US. The image facade, I had developed out of survival mode. Did NOT protect Me; but weakened Me. Establishing and finding my VOICE, my identity and authenticity, was GOD'S Healing Mercy and Grace for and upon Me. I'm FOREVER Grate-FULL to have learned to; "Save My Life; NOT My Image."

My Autobiography and Contemporary Guide to Survivors of Sexual Abuse and Domestic Violence. Entitled; "Save Your Life, NOT Your Image." Is available online ONLY, at Barnes and Nobles and at Amazon.

Rising from the Ashes: My Journey from Darkness to Resilience
Elissa Gabrielle

The Beginning of Loss

Grief is a silent, relentless storm that sweeps through your life, leaving destruction and heartache in its wake. It is an emotion that shatters the foundation of your existence, leaving you lost and adrift in a world that suddenly feels unfamiliar and harsh. This is the story of how grief shattered my life when I lost my beloved father, Joe, and the arduous journey I undertook to overcome this adversity.

It's amazing that this book would refer to ashes. It's one of the many words my father used when he described me and our life together. He would say, "Lisa, you rose up out of the ashes." He would refer to devastating moments in my childhood to where God had brought me into my forties. It's miraculous when I think about it. It's all good and it's all God.

My journey through grief begins with a deep and unbreakable bond between my father and me. From my earliest memories, Joe was more than just a parent; he was my hero, my confidant, and my unwavering source of support. He had a magical way of making me feel like the most special person in the world, and his belief in me was a constant source of motivation. We spent countless hours together during my childhood, exploring the outdoors, learning about nature, and developing a profound love for the world around us. Those days were filled with laughter, adventure, and the pure joy of being in each other's company. My father nurtured my curiosity, teaching me life's most important lessons through our shared experiences.

I had always been a Daddy's girl. My father, Joe Thomas, was my hero, my confidant, and my source of unwavering support. He had a way of making me feel like the most special person in the world, and he never missed an opportunity to remind me of my worth. As a child, I spent countless hours with him, exploring the jazz and its artists, learning about words and sounds, and developing a deep love for music and the world around me.

My father, Joe Thomas, was a well-known jazz musician. He recorded nine albums in his career. He never quite achieved stardom – the kind that his talent should have garnered. That didn't stop him from being a superstar in my eyes.

Our bond only grew stronger as I grew older. Joe was there for me during every milestone, from my first day of school to my high school graduation. He encouraged me to pursue all of my dreams and supported me through the ups and downs of life. My father was my rock, and I couldn't imagine a world without him.

But then, one fateful day, everything changed. I received a call that would shatter my world into a million pieces. My father had fallen, while simply walking across the street. I'd learn over the next day or so that he had suffered his second stroke. Rushing to the hospital, I clung to the hope that he would pull through, that our time together was not yet over. The news wasn't grim but became increasingly devastating over the next ten months.

A Heartbreaking Farewell

The hospital room was cold and sterile, a stark contrast to the warmth and love that had always surrounded me and my father. As I entered the room, I was met with a sight that left me breathless. Tubes and machines surrounded him, and the sound of monitors beeping filled the air. My father was all smiles and full of jokes as usual. I smiled with my heart. There was hope.

I've always known that nursing homes are the vortex to death. Over the next several months, my father's health continued to deteriorate. He fought a valiant fight. The same way he did when he fought in the Korean war. He was awarded the Purple Heart for his bravery. He was so brave during this heartbreaking time.

I received a phone call at 8:30pm on July 26th. I was told my father passed away. I didn't go to the hospital. I waited until he was brought to the funeral home to see him. My father lay motionless, his face was full, handsome as he always was. He was sleep. Peacefully.

On the inside, I could barely comprehend the words. My father was dead. It was as if the ground had been ripped out from beneath my feet. My father, the man who had always been so full of life and laughter, now hung on the edge of death.

Prior to his death, days turned into weeks as I sat by my father's bedside, praying for a miracle. Friends and family came to offer their support, but nothing could fill the void that was growing inside me. I held onto the memories of our time together, replaying them like a broken record in my mind.

Then, one fateful night, as I held my father's frail hand, he whispered his final words, "I love you, Elissa." Tears streamed down my face as I watched the light in his eyes fade away. I knew death would come soon, and my father would leave me alone in the darkness of grief.

The Abyss of Grief

My world crumbled in the wake of my father's death. The pain was unbearable, a constant ache that gnawed at my heart. I wasn't visibly distraught. I didn't want my children to see me broken. However, I withdrew from my friends, my work, and the world at large. Every day felt like a struggle just to breathe, and the weight of my sorrow threatened to consume me entirely.

I tried to make sense of the loss, but the questions haunted me: Why did this happen? Why was my father taken from me so suddenly? What was the purpose of life if it could be extinguished in an instant? The answers eluded me, leaving me feeling adrift in a sea of despair.

My grief manifested in different ways. I couldn't sleep, haunted by nightmares of my father's death. Then on the contrary, I slept too much. Food lost its taste, and I had no appetite. Then food tasted too good. Even the things I used to love, like hiking in the woods or reading a good book or writing – the gift of the written word my father gave me, held no appeal anymore.

A Ray of Hope

Months passed, and my grief showed no sign of relenting. But in the midst of my despair, a glimmer of hope emerged. I went to God. He guided me to read stories of others who had lost a loved one. I listened to interviews, podcasts, and stories from my handful of friends. As I listened to the stories of others who had experienced profound loss, something remarkable happened. I realized and was reminded that I wasn't alone in my suffering, that there were others who understood the depths of my grief.

Others strength and resilience inspired me, and my relationship with God blossomed. I began to lean on each Him, sharing my stories of remembrance, my tears, and my hopes for a brighter future.

The Healing Journey Begins

It was a slow process, but I began to confront the pain and trauma I had been avoiding. I learned that it was okay to grieve, to feel anger, guilt, and sadness. And most importantly, I learned that healing was possible.

I started to journal my feelings, pouring my heart out onto the pages. Writing became a therapeutic outlet, it was cathartic, allowing me to express the emotions that had been trapped inside for so long. It was in those private moments of reflection that I began to find a sense of peace.

Embracing Change

As time passed, I realized my father would want me to live a life filled with purpose and happiness. Deciding to honor his memory by embracing the lessons he had taught me about the beauty of the natural world. I returned to my childhood love of nature, spending more time outdoors, hiking, and exploring the wilderness. I also returned to jazz. Music filled my home once again. The rhythm of the sax, the high hat and bass had the house jumping, just like it did growing up in Newark, New Jersey, the same way it did every Christmas in the Poconos where we would welcome my Dad with open arms for a week of family, food and fun.

In the midst of my healing journey, I also reconnected with my friends and family, opening myself up to the support and love they had to offer. Although, I'm not certain they really knew I was gone. I found solace in the small moments of connection, like sharing a meal with loved ones or simply sitting in comfortable silence.

A New Beginning

Years have passed, and my life has life transformed in ways I could never have imagined during the darkest days of my grief. I channeled my pain into a passion for helping others who had experienced loss, becoming an advocate for mental health and grief support. I volunteered at a local women's shelter, offering a compassionate ear to those in need.

I began to involve myself heavily in what I call "Soul work." I gave myself to others in a way that would be life-affirming. Through my journey, I learned that resilience wasn't about erasing the pain of loss but about finding the strength to carry it and transform it into something meaningful. I realized that life was a series of ups and downs, and while the pain of my father's loss would always be a part of me, it no longer defines me.

My journey through grief has been a tumultuous one, marked by pain, despair, and ultimately, resilience. The loss of my father shattered my world, but it also taught me that the human spirit is remarkably resilient. I learned that healing is not a linear path, but a series of peaks and valleys.

Grief will always be a part of my life, but it no longer defines me. I have emerged from the darkness with a renewed sense of purpose, a deeper understanding of the human experience, and an unwavering commitment to helping others navigate their own journeys of grief. Through my story, I hope to inspire and encourage those who are struggling with loss to find their own path to healing and resilience.

In the end, it is the love and connections we build that sustain us through the darkest times, and it is the strength of the human spirit that allows us to rise from the ashes of grief and find a new beginning. My journey is a testament to the power of resilience, and a reminder that even in our darkest moments, there is hope for a brighter tomorrow.

Meet Elissa Gabrielle

Empowering, Enlightening, Engaging and Inspirational, Elissa Gabrielle is a powerhouse in the literary industry. Respected by many, revered in the highest regard, Elissa Gabrielle maintains a spirit of excellence in all she does. She is known to have the midas touch. The sky is the limit for this sassy, sundry and prolific author. Elissa Gabrielle has broken the ceiling of literary excellence with her gift in the skill of multi-genre writing. The author of multiple poetry books, numerous novels and contributor to several anthologies, Elissa has proven herself to be well-versed in artistic creativity.

Elissa Gabrielle has published close to 200 books and launched the literary careers of more than 30 authors in her 18-year career as an independent publisher. She has also won prestigious awards over the years. Elissa Gabrielle hails from Newark, New Jersey where she was born and raised. Elissa Gabrielle is a National Best-Selling Author, Publisher, Screenwriter, Producer, Brand Ambassador, Certified Natural Health Professional and Certified Life Coach.

Elissa Gabrielle is a producer for the forthcoming documentary, "Unheard Voices." The documentary covers the profile in courage of mother, author and entrepreneur, Tosha Smith Mills and her mission surrounding mothers of incarcerated children.

Elissa Gabrielle has the uncanny ability to take newcomers and mold, shape them into literary superstars and has created multiple award-winning authors and best-selling books in the process. Elissa Gabrielle's award-winning novel Eye of the Beholder was recommended by USA TODAY and she won Female Author of the Year for the novel by the African American Literary Awards. Her colloquial and imaginative creations have led to sensual and seductive inclusions in Zane's Purple Panties, Erogenous Zone: A Sexual Voyage, Mocha Chocolate: A Taste of Ecstasy, The Heat of the Night, Historie Chocolate D'Amour, Pillow Talk in the Heat of The Night, Zane's Busy Bodies: Chocolate Flava 4 and more.

But, Elissa Gabrielle is so much more…

As a Literary Entrepreneur, Elissa is the founder of the former greeting card line, Greetings from the Soul: The Elissa Gabrielle Collection, collaborator and creator of The Triumph of My Soul, and publisher of Peace In The Storm Publishing. Elissa has managed to turn relatively unknown authors into household names and has molded and shaped the careers of some of today's brightest literary stars. In addition to these innovative achievements, Elissa has graced the covers of Victorious Living Magazine, The Celebrity Online Magazine, Conversations Magazine, Big Time Publishing Magazine, Black Girl Powerhouse Magazine, Disilgold Soul Magazine and has been featured in Urbania Magazine and Black Literature Magazine. Elissa Gabrielle has also been featured in the Huffington Post and Madame Noire.

Peace In The Storm Publishing and Elissa Gabrielle have been nominated in over 30 literary awards and have won multiple awards individually and collectively for the publishing house, include the 2020 Independent Publisher of the Year Award for the 16th Annual African American Literary Awards. In 2015, Peace In The Storm Publishing expanded to include additional publishing imprints: After the Storm Publishing, Jessica A. Robinson Presents, Imani Faith Publishing, and the former, The Imprint Mass Media. The latest imprint is Renewing Your Mind Ink. Elissa Gabrielle is also the President of the former Real Life Real Faith Media. In that role, Elissa publishes five magazines: Real Life Real Faith, Men of Faith, Women Walking by Faith, Journey to Wellness and Wisdom for Everyday Life.

In 2020, Elissa Gabrielle turned pain into purpose by launching Elissa Gabrielle Naturals. Initially the brand will focus on hair care, and in following with Elissa's experience as a certified life coach and certified natural health professional, Elissa Gabrielle Naturals will launch skin care, health and wellness seminars, life coaching and naturopathic services under the Dr. Elissa brand in the future.

An advocate for Black Men, Elissa Gabrielle often brings awareness to the positive influences that embodies the black men in society that deserve a spotlight. She vigorously and unapologetically celebrates the unsung hero. She has taken this mission to publishing with The Soul of a Man series which details and highlights the plights, trials and triumphs of black men in their own words and from their very unique perspective.

From the novelty of her writing and the successful culmination of her publishing and entertainment companies; Elissa Gabrielle remains an ingenious and creative force to be reckoned with in terms of delivering distinct, fulfilling and entertaining literature. By pushing herself to stay a cut above the rest, Elissa Gabrielle brilliantly and consistently delivers literary best.

Living My Life, Despite the Pain
Jamesina Greene

Very often, I speak with individuals who are experiencing major life changes, due to sudden physical limitations and dysfunction. Whether it is because of surgeries or diseases, the consistent complaint is that they feel forgotten, dismissed, and misunderstood. Quite often, the circle of friends and family members seem to distance themselves as they continue on their individual life journeys. The phone calls and visits begin to slow down and sometimes come to an end. Those with whom you have been bonded, seem to forget that while you may have a "new normal" you desire that your relationships remain intact. The fact that you now have physical limitations or disabilities does not diminish your value or worth. There are a few physical pains that can match the pain of feeling unloved and unwanted.

This phase of my Journey began with the deaths of my world foundation, my Parents. In December 2010, I received a phone call that literally threw my world off course. I actually lost consciousness for a while. My Daddy was gone! He passed while in the Hospital for a condition that he had been there for multiple times, and he always came home. I did not expect this time to be any different. When the Doctor called me with the news, EVERYTHING shifted. Once I was able to function again, it hit me that it was my youngest son's 18th birthday. Oh my God, how was I going to tell this boy that his Pop-Pop was gone AND on his birthday! Somehow, I made it to his friend's house where he was staying and shared the horrible news with him. As expected he was devastated. He went into a deep depression and his Senior Year in High School was his worst year ever. He had four different College invites, and they were pursuing him hard; however, after this event, his grades, attendance, and attitude changed, and the calls and letters stopped coming.

Needless to say, as the epitome of a "Daddy's Girl" I could

not even imagine how to proceed without my Daddy. Having already been diagnosed with Major Depression and Anxiety Disorder, people were saying that this would push me over the edge, and I would most likely end up in a long-term Mental Health Facility. They had no clue about the strength that I possessed and to be honest, neither did I. I reached out to my Therapist and as usual, she helped walk me through the worst days. Another admission was not needed.

As I was doing what I could to deal with Daddy's death and its impact on my children and grandchildren, I had also been living with my Parents for approximately 1 year as their Caregiver. Mom had Alzheimer's Disease and Heart Disease, while Daddy had Heart Disease and other chronic illnesses. It was a very stressful time, but I loved them and would do whatever I could for them.

The day that Daddy died, Mom stopped talking. She would make a moaning sound but would no longer say words. The Doctor said that even though her mental capacity was altered, she knew that her Husband of almost 50 years was gone. Three days before she transitioned, she called his name and the name of my sister who had transitioned six years earlier. She went to join them exactly three months and three days after Daddy.

In the midst of the pain, I also felt a sense of relief. My Parents were no longer sick and suffering. I could begin to focus on my delayed dreams and goals, while encouraging and nudging my son to do the same. I understood that it would not be easy, but it was possible. So, we both began our path to healing and moving forward. I convinced him to go to College and slowly build himself back up. A year later, it all went off track again.

I was living with a family member, and it was a very uncomfortable situation. I began having even more health issues than before, including major headaches and severe neck pain. I remember walking to an Employment Office with the intention of following up on some online postings. As I entered the reception area, the Receptionist asked me for my name and social security number so that she could pull up my file. The next thing I remember was being in the back of an ambulance as the EMT was trying to rip my fingernails off. I heard someone tell her to stop because they were my real nails, not press-ons!

The next conscious moment was the ER Doctor telling me that I had had a stroke and was being admitted. During my time there, it was determined that over the years, the vertebrae in my neck had fused together and cracked. This caused my already high blood pressure to go even higher and caused the stroke. A surgical procedure called a "Spinal Fusion" was needed. The first Spinal Fusion was performed and when I came out of the OR, my left side was paralyzed, and I could not speak clearly. I could not remember words or how to use them. I was terrified, yet I had a feeling that I was going to be okay. After a few days in the Hospital, post-surgery, I was transferred to a local Nursing Home/Rehabilitation Center for care. While there, I had to learn how to walk and talk again. When I was discharged from there, I continued with Home Health Care, including Nursing, Physical Therapy, Occupational Therapy, and Speech Therapy.

As I continued improving in these areas, the pain in my neck was getting worse, even with the neck braces that I wore. In addition, I was assigned a Personal Care Aide to help with bathing, dressing, laundry, etc., but outside of the hours that the Aide was there, I was most left alone and isolated, lying in a hospital bed in the bedroom. Depression was a constant companion.

During one of my follow-up visits to my Surgeon, I expressed my concern regarding the neck pain, and he sent me to have an MRI. A couple of weeks later, I went in for another follow-up and once again, my world shifted. While he was looking at the MRI, a really strange look came over his face and he was staring intensely at it for several minutes. Finally, I asked was there a problem. He pointed out to me that one of the screws had come out of the metal plate implanted in my neck; the plate was slightly twisted because of that and therefore, the Fusion was not happening. He also mentioned that he was surprised that I was able to function so well, because technically, my neck and spine were not being held together properly! Hence the excruciating pain.

I was not even allowed to go back home. I had to go straight from his Office to the Hospital for admission. Three and a half months after the first Spinal Fusion Surgery, I was back in the OR for a 2-1/2 procedure that would last ten hours. During that procedure, my jugular vein was nicked, and they lost me twice on the operating table, because they could not stop the bleeding. Ultimately, a Vascular Surgeon was called in to tie off some veins in my neck area before the Neurosurgeon could continue.

As a result of botched surgeries and misdiagnosis, I have often felt like calling it quits. Many times, I was told that it was a burden for family and friends to help with my daily care and I felt it would be better for everyone if I was dead. I began preparing to die instead of looking forward to living. I sat down and wrote out my wishes for my Funeral and began writing letters to be read to my sons and grandsons after my death. Emotionally, physically, and spiritually, I felt completely pained and useless. I was ready to just leave everything, the pain, and the triumphs.

But the Creator revealed that there was more living for me to do. Suddenly and consistently, I started hearing from individuals how my life was encouraging and inspiring them. Those who had lost parents were motivated to turn those memories into treasures as they heard me talk about and honor my parents. Mothers whose hearts had been ripped to pieces, leaving them feeling helpless as their sons became a statistic in the mass incarceration and prison industrial complex of the United States, began following my story. They saw and felt my spoken words and advocacy in a fight against a Country and system that incarcerates more people than any country in the entire world.

In addition, many people who suffer with chronic illnesses, for which there are no cures, reached out to me for prayer and advice. They informed me that my transparency, honesty, and humor while dealing with the pain from my illnesses, helped them to shift focus. From watching and interacting with me, they learned that their illnesses are not the sum total of who they are. They choose to live life.

Slowly but surely, I began to recognize and accept my Purpose. I found my Voice in the midst of what I believed was a barren and unproductive season of life. Oh yeah, speaking of my voice. I was told by medical professionals that because of what happened during that second surgery, I would most likely never be able to speak above a whisper and there would be some trouble with speaking clearly. I would not be understood by many people. As I found my voice, spiritually, it began to strengthen physically. This is one of the main reasons that I began my Virtual Talk Show. I am determined to use my voice, no matter how it sounds.

Today, I can say with total honesty that I am living in spite of the pain and because of it. I use my pain and painful experiences as fuel for my passion. I am not going to waste the pain; I'm going to use it. I AM moving forward in victory and anticipating some great days ahead!

Meet Jamesina Greene

Jamesina Greene is a powerful voice focused on honesty and advocacy. Founder of "A Mother's Cry" a community-based outreach organization supporting families impacted by social inequalities and injustices. including the immediate need for prison reform in this Country.

She is also Founder of the following entities: the "Let's Talk Destne Talk Show;" J.E.G. Marketplace Ministry and the Redemptive Brilliance brand. Always encouraging the pursuit of one's purpose, Jamesina is known as the "Purpose Advocate." Also, an award-winning Author; a playwright; songwriter; blogger and content creator.

Loving Mother and Grandmother, Jamesina is a voice for those who feel voiceless. Her perseverance through extensive loss and illness is inspiration for many.

CONTACT:
https://www.Facebook.com/AMothersCry61
https://www.Instagram.com/amotherscry_61
https://www.Twitter.com/jamee_am1
Destne2017@gmail.com
Amcjami@gmail.com
https://www.youtube.com/channel/UCcuwUN-OdR0kN70jyFpev3A

Afraid to Live and Afraid to Die
Sharel E. Gordon-Love

"As soon as you get out of here, I want you to see an oncologist," the surgeon stated after he had finished admiring his surgical handiwork and the wound that he said showed no signs of infection. What he did not say was that he cut me from the bottom of my stomach up to just under my breasts.

"Okay," I answered, not allowing the word "oncologist" to register in my psyche. *This man must be out of his mind*, I thought to myself. My father died from lung cancer almost four years prior, and there was no way I was going to see an oncologist so I could be treated with chemotherapy and radiation. No thanks! I would just live as long as I could and…well actually, I did not have a plan. The fear of going to see an oncologist was more than enough for me to ignore this doctor.

The doctor was obviously shocked by my nonchalant response, so he said, "Let me tell you what we found during surgery. You had five carcinoid tumors in your intestines, the biggest one was blocking them completely. We had to remove a foot of the intestines, along with your appendix because it was trapped by scar tissue. If we did not remove that, you would have been right back in here. We had to check all your major organs and internal parts of your body to see if it had metastasized, but there was no sign of it. I still would like for you to see an oncologist right away, and I will refer you to someone when you are discharged." Mind you, he never said it was cancer straight out or what carcinoid even meant, and I made a point of not asking him to elaborate.

My response? "Okay."

I saw this surgeon six days straight, and each day he would remind me to see an oncologist, and each day my response was the same. On one of my walks through the hospital hallways, I decided to venture around to the other side on the same floor and came upon a ward of patients that looked like they were in different phases of cancer treatment and yet dying. Reading a sign, I realized that this was where people suffering from terminal cancer were being treated, and I almost passed out. It finally registered: I have cancer.

Each day of my hospital stay, I was asked had I used the bathroom and did not know until a month later that using the bathroom would plague me for years to come due to having a lower bowel resection and how that bodily function would affect my life.

On the 6th day of my hospital stay, the doctor released me to go home on Christmas Day, 2007. My two youngest sons finished the setup of my bedroom since we were in a new residence. That evening I was able to rest comfortably in my bed and slept well in between the pain medication.

At first, I did not tell my sons about the cancer diagnosis because their father had just successfully beat cancer, and his treatment included chemotherapy. The fear I saw in their eyes convinced me that I should not tell them, although they were young adults in their 20s. Their father's diagnosis caused them to view life differently, and I did not want to take them through another parent's seriously ill journey.

Finally, I told them when I had to go to my primary care doctor who is a man of faith. He told me I was looking at six weeks of chemotherapy to start, and my response was, "I do not want chemo...I watched how it destroyed my father before he passed away from lung cancer, and I know I cannot handle it."

"What you need to do is believe God for your first miracle of 2008."

"Okay, I will because I do not want to go through that." I

left there with a referral to an oncologist whose practice I still go to today, with fear right up under the surface while my prayer consisted of only the following four words consistently: "I do not want chemo." I could not pray anything else to save me; there was nothing else to be said.

Before the testing began, I went and sat with my pastor and told him everything the doctors told me and what I had to go through. He told me I had to believe what I asked God for, and then he prayed for me before I left his office. That evening I had a dream that I was at church during a service, and I praised God with all my heart. I told my youngest son's Godmother that I wanted to live. Still, fear had a way of rising out of nowhere because I knew that I was diagnosed with cancer; so surreal.

When I went to see the oncologist, the nurse that drew my blood told me that most times they can tell the cause of cancer by where it is located. Unfortunately, the doctor I saw told me that they do not know what causes carcinoid cancer, only that it is in the digestive tract. Not only that, it is rare, and most people have one tumor, but I had five! Truth be told I made the medical books because this does not happen did not encourage me at all. That scared me even more…now what? Well, testing that would take three days of scans called an octreotide scan.

The first day of testing I arrived at the facility at 6:00 in the morning to have the medication administered via I.V. that would take a few hours to circulate through my body. Mind you, everyone that was in the room with me assisting put on hazard protection. I was speechless…even when the doctor spilled some of the medication on her scrubs, she hurried to change. I thought, *if it is that hazardous, why are they putting it in me?* I couldn't even get that question out.

I went back home and did a few things, then had lunch with the person that took me to my visit. We sat in my kitchen and talked until it was time for us to return to the facility for the first scan. I ended up falling asleep while lying in the machine because of the pain medication and the fact that it took 3 to 3.5 hours for the scan to be completed. I had to return the next two days in a row with the final scan not being as long, but the naps still happened.

A few days later while I was at another doctor's appointment, the oncologist called and let my mother know that I was not only cancer-free, but there was none detected in my whole body! Hallelujah! If I could have run around my house after my mother told me the news, I would have. But as I lay in my bed because I was so exhausted, I raised my hands and voice in praise to God, it was all I could do. I was still walking bent over and needed the pain medication far longer than I anticipated.

My recovery was slower than I expected, although I was not ready to return to work. My mother was right by my side, literally nursing me back to health from drinking everything until it was time to begin adding solid food back into my diet. The surgery changed cold drinks to warm or room temperature because I could feel the trail of anything cold. My children teased me then, but I do drink my water at room temperature today.

The other thing that I am sure caused my recovery to be slower is, I refused to let go of the staples. I believe that subconsciously I felt my incision did not heal enough to keep everything inside since it was so long. I kept telling the surgeon I was seeing in New Jersey that the incision was not fully healed. He let me have my way for a while, but finally on one visit, he told me they had to go, at which time he put surgical tape over the whole incision. I still felt like something was going to fall out of the middle of my gut.

Returning to work in April of 2008, half days for six weeks wasn't too bad, and going back full-time worked for a little while. By the end of July, I found myself constantly praying about leaving work permanently. Whatever was going on in my body was beginning to take a toll on me, and I was dragging. By September, I spoke to our HR administrator, and my primary physician, and together, they helped transition me to becoming legally disabled.

In addition to the cancer diagnosis, my joints began to hurt terribly, and although the doctor told me he believed I had rheumatoid arthritis, the blood work came back negative. By this time, my company-provided insurance was ending, and I found myself without any for a while thereafter. Since I could not find affordable coverage, and neither did I qualify for state provided insurance, I had to find medical coverage somehow. Instead, I found myself at a clinic covered by charity care with a doctor that was only interested in the medications I was currently on, and what he could give me for any other ailments. The only time he became concerned is when my blood work came back showing that my iron count was 4 instead of 12.

Around this time is when I found myself in a deep depression that I could not pull myself out of. I put on a good face when I left the house, if I had to leave the house, but otherwise my bed would become my constant companion. Up in the morning, shower, change my pajamas, grab a cup of coffee, watch court shows, and take a nap after lunch. It seemed I could not catch a break; every time I started planning to get up and do something with my life, with my ministry, surgery came and knocked me back down. What did I do? I stayed down and convinced myself that I should stay on the sidelines and cheer my sons on as they grew in God and in ministry.

Those naps? They were my escape from my life, my reality that I no longer wanted to be part of or deal with. Each day I worried about the reoccurrence of cancer and ultimately, death. So, I slept for hours every day. My thought process was I could sleep from this world right into eternity not knowing anything until I arrived there. Yet, a part of my feared dying and leaving my sons because I wanted to be part of who they were becoming as men. I held on by meeting God in His house on Sunday mornings. I put a smile on my face no matter how bad I was feeling, praised God, felt a little better than when I arrived there, and enjoyed it until the next day.

It was also during this time that I received a call from a friend stating that a pastor and local radio owner wanted to meet with me at 3:00 that afternoon. Mind you, I had just hung up with her saying I was about to take a nap. When she called back, I picked up and didn't say 'hello,' I simply said, 'no.' Explaining it was not her idea to ask me, I reminded her thar it was my nap time and I had to go. She called right back at the pastor's insistence, so I agreed to go not knowing it would be pivotal to turnaround I needed for my life.

Out of this encounter, I had an opportunity to work at a radio station, have my own radio broadcast, "Inspired Moments With Sharel," and work behind the scenes with an MLM company. I learned a lot, but more than anything, I learned that I could face the reality of my health, and in turn, do something about it. Accepting what the doctors had been telling me is where I started, the medications and a true search of their side effects was another, and finally a true commitment to taking care of my health.

This one opportunity changed the trajectory of my life and I have not looked back since. I have since had gall bladder surgery, surgery for a reoccurrence from carcinoid cancer (and did not need chemotherapy or radiation), a laminectomy, two microscopic knee surgeries, a complete left hip surgery, a few foot surgeries, one very extensive, and a spinal stimulator. I have wires, leads and a battery in my back as well as an external battery I must carry at all times.

Depression became a thing of the past when the Lord told me that I am "Limitless Through My Limitedness." No longer am

I afraid to die because living meant death at every turn.

Meet Sharel E. Gordon-Love

Sharel E. Gordon-Love is a licensed evangelist, author, publisher, motivational speaker, and brand ambassador who is a former Domestic Violence victim and a two-time cancer survivor. Sharel personally advocates for both her writing and the platform of inspirational speaker to share her experiences and life journey.

Sharel will tell you that as a child, life was never ordinary for her. It was during these formative years that she found a great love for the written word and the vehicle it is to be able to help and encourage others.

Born and raised in Plainfield, New Jersey, Evangelist Love is the oldest daughter born to the late Ronald A. Gordon, and Coretha Cobb. She is the mother of three sons, Khayree, Alvin "AJ," and Ronald, (Tamare), and grandmother to identical twin girls, Harper and Olivia.

Sharel E. Gordon-Love, who has reviewed literary artists for A Place of Our Own Book Club (APOOO) 2005 to 2014, also hosted her own radio broadcast, "Inspired Moments with Sharel," at World Harvest Radio located in Plainfield, New Jersey. She enjoyed using this platform to introduce new authors, singers, poets, artists, and activists, who, like her, address critical health concerns, and work to bring about social change.

Writing for Sharel began at the age of six, winning immediate recognition for her essays and short stories. Her first nonfiction work, "Is There Hope for the Black Male?" was published by Black Child Magazine in 1994.

Sharel's life experiences and formal education is what she pulled from as an author through which she has been part of an anthology, titled The Heart of Our Community in 2006. Additionally, Sharel has several published works beginning with the "Seasons of Life" Sharel has also released a 7-book eBook series titled, "Saved to Served."

In July of 2015, Sharel became the publisher of After The Storm Publishing, LLC, a division of Peace in the Storm Publishing, LLC. ASP Kids, the children's division of After The

Storm Publishing launched July of 2017.

Becoming a brand ambassador for Elissa Gabriele Naturals in 2019, Sharel shares her experience with the product line and the growth of her natural hair that healed her scalp and generated growth in areas of hair loss and damage. She was able to regrow her hair with this product after contracting COVID-19 in March of 2020 when her hair fell out as well. She is also an ambassador for Allure Views, a company that makes casual workout gear and clothing.

A dedicated Christian, and active church worker on her local and jurisdictional church administrative staff, youth department, and women's ministries, Sharel is also a licensed evangelist missionary in the Church of God in Christ, where she, along with family, attend New Reid Temple COGIC, in East Orange, New Jersey.

Sharel, resides in North Plainfield, New Jersey with her family.

*

A Black Girl's Rebirth
Armani Peterson

In the shadowed depths of darkest night,
She emerged, a beacon, a guiding light.
A woman of strength, her spirit ablaze,
She conquered adversity in countless ways.

Through trials and tribulations, she did roam,
But she forged her path, found her way back home.
With courage in her heart, and fire in her soul,
She refused to let life's challenges take their toll.

The storms may have raged,
and the winds may have howled,
But she stood unyielding, her resolve unbowed.
In the face of adversity, she found her grace,
A testament to the beauty of her determined face.

With each obstacle she faced, she grew stronger still, Turning
setbacks into lessons, with unwavering will.
She climbed every mountain, crossed every sea,
For she believed in the power of her destiny.

No burden too heavy, no hurdle too high,
She reached for the stars, touching the sky.
From the depths of despair to triumphant delight,
She emerged as a beacon, a shining light.

Her story inspires, her journey inspires,
A testament to the human spirit's fires.
In the face of adversity, she found her way,
Triumphing in life, come what may.

So let her story be a lesson to us all,
That in the face of adversity, we can stand tall.
With strength and courage, we too can thrive,
And overcome all obstacles in this grand, precious life.

In the heart of darkness, where shadows cast their pall,
A woman stood alone, amidst the ruins that did sprawl, The
remnants of a life once lived,
now shattered, torn, and frayed,
But in her eyes, a spark remained, a beauty yet unswayed.

For she had known the depths of pain,
the anguish, and despair,
Yet within her, there burned a fire,
a hope beyond compare.
She looked upon the ashen landscape,
where others saw but blight,
And in those ashes,
she discerned a glimmer of pure light.

The world had dealt its harshest blows,
with trials and with tests,
But from the depths of suffering,
she'd risen from the nests.
In every broken piece,
she saw a chance to start anew,
To build a life more beautiful,
and to dreams, she would stay true.

With hands once stained by tears,
now reaching for the sky,
She vowed to craft a future where her spirit could truly fly. In
each shattered fragment, she uncovered hidden grace,
A testament to the resilience that lit her path and pace.

She found beauty in the ashes,
in the wreckage and the pain,
A strength born from adversity,
like sunshine after rain.
For scars may mark the surface,
but they tell a tale of strength,
And in her journey's tapestry,
there lay a breadth and length.

The lessons learned in hardship,
in the crucible of strife,
Forged her into something new,
a woman full of life.
The scars and ashes were but symbols of her phoenix's ascent, A
story of rebirth and beauty
from a life that once was spent.

With every step she took, on the road to healing's grace, She
found more than restoration;
she discovered her own place.
No longer bound by sorrow,
no longer held by chains,
She walked with newfound purpose,
where beauty ever reigns.

And as the years passed by, the ashes turned to earth, Beneath
her feet, they crumbled, giving rise to rebirth.
A garden bloomed where once was naught
but dust and pain,
A testament to her spirit, her strength,
her love, her gain.

So, let her story be a testament, a beacon in the night,
That even from the darkest depths, one can find their light. For
in the ashes of despair, beauty can arise,
A testament to the human spirit's boundless, endless skies.